# Forgetting

## STORIES BY
## KAREN HEULER

Published by Bitingduck Press
ISBN 978-1-938463-33-4
eISBN 978-1-68553-003-7
© 2022 Karen Heuler
All rights reserved
For information contact
Bitingduck Press, LLC
Altadena, CA
notifications@bitingduckpress.com
http://www.bitingduckpress.com
Cover photo by Lynn Gallagher-Ford

# Forgetting

## STORIES BY
# KAREN HEULER

*This is the Hour of Lead —*
*Remembered, if outlived,*
*As Freezing persons, recollect the Snow—*
*First—Chill—then Stupor— then the letting go –*
                                    *Emily Dickinson*

# CONTENTS

# 1

# SEARCHING FOR PENNY

QUITE SUDDENLY, IT SEEMED to Grace, her mother had suffered a stroke, which meant that she had trouble talking and was weak along her right side. At first it was scary, but when her mother started smiling—even if it was only half her face that was smiling—it seemed that life would be different, but good.

Her mother held her hand out a lot now, her good hand, her left hand. Her right hand sometimes weighed too much. "Oo vat," her mother said once, and Grace understood her. Her arm felt too fat.

Grace's father got some aides to come in and work with her mother for a while (just till she got back to normal), and life became routine again. Grace visited a few times a week to sit with her and after a while she started reading to her mother, just as her mother used to read to her.

Memories of childhood led to memories of her mother helping her with books of cutout dolls who came with cutout clothes and cutout furniture. Her mother's therapist emphasized tasks that involved the hands, so Grace went to children's stores and found a book with cutout castles with tabs to bend and interlock so the walls could stand up on their own. She honestly thought her mother would enjoy them, and it seemed she did, though her smile was too crooked to read correctly. "It's ironic, not funny," she told her mother. "I mean, me helping you with things you once helped me with. Must feel strange."

Her mother was quiet for a moment, holding a pair of large, blunt scissors in her hand loosely, dropping them often. "Everything is strange," she said finally, though it came out sounding like "eh-ing ith stange."

Grace was pleased when a rickety paper-thin castle finally stood between them. Her mother had done a few of the tabs; it seemed a small triumph, and she stuck her hand out in congratulations. But her mother's movements were clumsy and abrupt, her hand like a mitt, and a sudden awkward movement sent her fist crashing down on the castle.

She gasped, then drew her hand back and bowed her head. "Ruined everything," she said, her "R's" still blocked and a few spare tears overflowing her eyes.

"My fault. Flimsy. Just paper, after all." Grace fingered it dismissively. "Why don't we just build whatever we want? Any way we want?" She looked brightly at her mother, who was staring miserably down at the ruined castle.

"Okay," she said, and Grace wasn't sure she wanted to, or just wanted to stop Grace from discussing it.

It was good for her mother's coordination, Grace decided; they would do it.

❖ ❖ ❖

SHE GOT FOAM BOARD, oak tag, glue, shish kebob sticks, popsicle sticks and colored felts and crayons and little jars of paints. She took it all to the back porch, an enclosed room with large screened windows that looked out on a long, narrow yard with a small patch of hydrangea and forsythia and dispirited grass. The forsythia had recently dropped its yellow blooms; it was May.

She set up the wooden table as a workspace, clearing off old magazines and bags of sno-melt and birdseed, and spread out her oak tag, the property on which she would lay out the house they would build together. She heard the uneven shuffle as her mother found her. When she walked she held her right arm in her left hand, to keep from hitting against walls or bric-a-brac, she said, though there was no bric-a-brac. But there were walls.

"What's this?" she asked. Grace was getting better at understanding her.

"We're going to build a house," Grace answered eagerly. She felt her own stupid smile on her face. Why should it be so pleasing, building a miniature house? "We can design it any way we like. As many rooms as we like. Windows and doors. And floors, too, as many as we want."

Her mother made it into her chair and sat down resignedly. She stared at the table. One side of her mouth drooped down dramatically, as did the left lower eyelid, still. She sat for a few minutes, looking down at the materials, and then out the windows and back again. Finally she shifted in her seat and said, "One floor. Ranch." She leaned on her good left hand and sat to Grace's right.

"Okay, good!" Grace said. "Where's the house?" she asked and then drew in a lightly penciled rectangle where her mother signaled. "Here it is, then," she said. "Garage?"

"Left side."

"Front path?"

"Yes."

Grace moved sticks around as her mother answered questions until finally her mother's good arm lifted up to support her head, which tilted to the side even when she wasn't weary, and now seemed to be on the verge of falling off. She stared out the window as Grace talked about school projects when she was very small, with her mother helping her make a map of the U.S., drawing in the borders with a firm hand. Only now her mother's right hand folded itself halfway to a fist, and it wandered vaguely, like a kitten taking its first few steps.

❈ ❈ ❈

"YOUR MOTHER'S DOING WELL, all things considered," her father said.

"I think so too. She's walking better. And her words aren't so slurred, unless she's tired."

"Yes," he said nodding. "Not quite what she was. But better." He had wandered into the kitchen, where Grace was making soups and casseroles to be frozen or plated in the refrigerator.

"You're working a lot, mom says." She had decided it would sound better if the observation came from her mother. In fact, Grace rarely saw him when she came in the evening. Her mother sat alone, kneading a rubber ball in her weak hand, watching TV.

"Not for much longer," he said. "We took on a new client just as one of the machines broke down. So we've been running pretty much round the clock to make it up." His father managed a metal sheeting company. "But we should be up and running with two new ones in a month or so." He paused, still standing on the other side of the room, away from her. "The timing was bad, I know, but I took off a lot when this happened. So I can't refuse. And the aide comes half a day. I make sure she's not alone for long."

"The aide is nice," she agreed. Her father was never a demonstrative man, but he used to be better; he used to place his hand on her shoulder. He looked at her thoughtfully, then said he had to leave and, as if reading her mind, touched her shoulder briefly, in passing.

She brought plates out to the porch, where her mother sat studying the diorama of the house. "He's gone?" her mother asked.

"Work," Grace answered.

"He doesn't know what to do with me." The good half of her face tried to look ironic.

Grace fought the urge to deny it, but she'd already wondered if that was it, if her father chose to work so much just to avoid her mother. He was not expressive; Grace knew that. She could fault him for it, but she was old enough to know that expecting people to change was ultimately unfair. Life wasn't giving her father the kind of problem he was good at. Was she herself good at it? She was spending more time with her mother than she should; she was married, after all (though she thought of it as being lightly married). Was she avoiding her own husband, or trying to make up for some guilt she felt towards her mother? The truth was that she saw her mother now as a different person. Well, then it wasn't true that people didn't change. Her mother had transformed into a person who had to learn a different physical language, a person whose body had become alien, and Grace was fascinated. This woman she'd always known was surprising her. And that, maybe, was where guilt came in: she preferred her mother this way.

It was obvious, for instance, that Grace enjoyed the role reversals. Here they were, essentially constructing a doll house, and Grace looked forward to her trips to Schachtman's, a toy store that specialized in miniatures for train sets and dolls' tea parties. She picked up foam bushes, plastic trees, meticulous little dressers and side tables, picturing the pleasure in her mother's face—or at least that new, acquiescent nod.

The diorama progressed nicely. Grace measured and cut out walls and floors, windows and doors. Her mother wanted to make curtains but she still couldn't use the scissors with her left hand, she held them all wrong. Once it had brought her to furious tears and Grace had hugged her mother, smoothing her hair and murmuring soothing sounds as her mother's back stiffened and she pulled away.

"Grace, don't treat me like a baby. You're patronizing me." It took her a long time to get the words out.

Grace dropped her head, as if her mother had slapped her hand. "I feel so bad for you," she said finally.

Her mother tried to hold her head high. "Don't."

In a few more days, her mother learned to use the scissors in her left hand. She didn't mention it; Grace noticed it and hid a faint smile.

Her mother said there should be a little bench by the front door; she made a doormat out of pipe cleaners, stained red with nail polish. Grace searched Schachtman's for a tiny piano and an old-fashioned TV.

One evening her father came out to the porch and watched them. By then, the house was in position—the front yard with a white-brick path, the layout of a garage to the side; the back was sketched in with a lawn, some bushes edging the sides, trees at the rear. And a little structure, a small room as her mother called it, tucked in nearly all the way down the right side in the back. The house itself had no roof so it was possible to look down into a living room and dining room near the front, a girl's bedroom to the left, and behind it a master bedroom.

Grace looked up at her father and smiled. He was studying the diorama. "Alice, it's your house," he said finally, to her mother. "Where you grew up. I recognize it."

A big smile creased her mother's face—the crease dividing the good right side and the sagging left side. "Home," she said. She pointed. "My room."

Her father leaned over a little. "I think I can see it," he said. "It's very good." He straightened up, his eyes traveling over the board. "What's that?" he asked, pointing to the little house at the rear of the property.

"Penny's house," her mother said. It took Grace a second to figure out what she'd said. She saw her father stiffen. "Penny?" Grace asked, and her mother nodded. Grace's eyes watched her father. She could almost see him processing—but what, she didn't know. Whatever it was, it had startled him. Who was Penny?

❖ ❖ ❖

The next time she came over, she found her father in the kitchen, drinking a beer. "You're home," she said in surprise.

"We got the equipment in ahead of time. I've been pushing as hard as I could." He ran a hand over his face. His eyes had loose skin under them. He took a great long drink from his beer.

"I have to ask you," she began. The name "Penny" had been building in her mind.

"Go to it."

"Are you having an affair?" she asked in a rush.

His eyebrows shot up; she thought the surprise was real. "Of course not," he said. "None of your business either."

"Then who's Penny?" she asked. "I got that right—Penny?"

He nodded, then put his beer down. "Penny was a little girl who disappeared when we were kids. She died. I don't know why your mother's thinking about her. I've made an appointment with the doctor. I don't know if it means anything."

❖ ❖ ❖

Her mother's speech improved; she was getting more adept at using her left hand, but she still dragged her right leg when she walked, and so she spent her time sitting. Brooding, Grace thought; grieving. Her father was home more often, and Grace came upon them sitting together silently, or watching the news, or eating. Her father brought food home, and then he learned, slowly, to cook. Or as Grace thought: fry. She hoped, in time, he would notice the oven, and the salad bowls. But for now, it was fine. She brought pastas and soups and artisanal breads.

For a time, the diorama stalled. She asked her mother once or twice if she wanted to work on it, but her mother looked at her slowly and shook her head. But Grace always went out to look at it, hoping it had changed a little. Was change the point? Was she really disappointed that her mother had lost interest in the gift she'd brought?

The doctor said she was having continuing small strokes, and it was affecting her mind as well as her body. She was on new medication. Her father didn't quite understand it, but the medicine should help her, at least in slowing down the progression of the strokes.

Her father settled back into his usual pattern; he fell asleep over a newspaper, or he read the paper at dinner. He told them about the latest practical joke at work—a world where dumb jokes were appreciated. She'd heard about them all her life.

And then her mother was back at the diorama when she came, and her father was back to working overtime.

"Oh?" she asked. "Has something happened?"

"It's hard, having him watching me. He shouldn't be looking for me."

Grace slipped into the chair next to her mother and they discussed where the trees should go.

"Dad doesn't mean to be looking at you," she said. "He wants to make sure you're okay. I do too." She patted her mother's hand. "I don't know how you're feeling. Will you tell me?" She had read up on the literature on how to talk to people like this: be simple, be direct, give them signs to understand things.

"I think I'm lost," her mother said. Her right eye got red and a tear stalled at the edge.

"If you ever got lost, we'd find you," Grace said. She thought it was good, talking in general terms.

Her mother's head moved slowly, her eyes dropped from their far-off vantage to glare at Grace. "You haven't heard a thing," she said softly. "You haven't heard me."

❊ ❊ ❊

HER MOTHER'S WORDS GOT her. Her mother, reaching out; and she'd misunderstood or missed it or simply couldn't sympathize. That was a terrible thing. She vowed to be more supportive, more imaginative in her support.

The next visit she found her father watching TV. "She's sleeping," he said, looking up at her.

"I think she's depressed or something." Grace sat down across from him.

"Sometimes I wonder," he said. "I don't know about depression, but she seems obsessed. About that well house, about Penny. Happened what—fifty years ago? And now it's an issue?" His eyebrows rose above his bleary eyes. "Do you understand that?"

What was there to understand? Something long ago was causing immense pain. Certainly, but why? She felt, at times, that her mother was making it up—wanting something from them she felt she wasn't getting.

"Tell me about Penny," she said. "What happened? How old were you?"

"I was 13. Your mother was 10. We lived within a block of each other. We went to the same school. Different grades, but it was a small school and at that time all the kids hung out on the street. Big kids picked on little kids, mocked them, tortured them, taught them things—no worse than anywhere else, and a lot better than kids have it today. At least we knew each other. We took it all for granted."

"Sounds wonderful."

"It was." He reached for the remote and turned off the TV, listening to the silence for a moment.

"The whole neighborhood searched for her, for three days, maybe four, I don't remember now. The kids went out in pairs—the grownups wouldn't allow children out alone. No one knew if she'd been abducted. Some people had seen a stranger in a car, you know how that goes. For those first days, there was always an adult on the street, no matter what, just standing on a porch or in a driveway, watching. Every child felt it, that sudden rise in value. I mean, we were all loved, I think, but now we were desired. You could feel it."

"So why is mom thinking about it?"

He shrugged, running his hand over his face. "I don't know. And I don't like it. It doesn't feel right. Does it feel healthy to you?"

She thought about it for a long time. "Maybe she's just going through memories, you know? Maybe she'll move on to something else."

❊ ❊ ❊

SHE DIDN'T MOVE ON. That place on the oak tag became a well house, *the* well house where Penny had been found. Her mother hummed as she completed it, and she grinned lopsidedly at Grace. Was it more lopsided? Her mother's left hand shook now. She leaned over the well house and made tender, cooing sounds.

"I think mom had another stroke," she said when her father came home. Her mother was sleeping. She usually slept for a few hours in the afternoon now.

He nodded. "I think so too. The doctor said she might."

"So soon?"

"It's not going to stop, Grace." His voice was tender.

Grace felt her heart tear, just a little. She felt a desperate need to understand what it meant. "Can you show me Penny's well house?" she asked. "The real one?"

He nodded. "Let's go while she's asleep."

❀ ❀ ❀

"These strokes," Grace said as they got in the car, "why can't they stop them?"

"They said they can't," he answered, starting the engine. "Should I argue with them? I've seen two doctors. She's going to keep having strokes, mostly small ones, if I understand right. Vascular dementia, it's called. I didn't believe them at first. I think I couldn't, at first."

"Dementia? She isn't crazy. I mean, yes, there are things. But she was getting better for a while."

They were leaving their neighborhood, going west, farther out from the center of town. There were more trees, larger lots. "Not better. I'm sorry. Not better; different. It hits her physically and mentally. Memory, motor skills, judgment." His hand gripped the steering wheel.

Grace stared out the window, letting the whipping change of details soothe her. The word *dementia* had cleared everything out of her head, leaving it wiped clean. She allowed one thing at a time back in. More strokes. Memory. Judgment.

"Can you get stuck on part of a memory?" she wondered. "Whatever it is, it seems to make her happy. Or something. Maybe 'happy' isn't the right word."

Her father sighed. "God knows it *shouldn't* be. It was awful. When you were little, just Penny's age, I went through a period where I couldn't put her out of my head. I watched everything you did. You remember Bruno?"

"What a great dog," she said. "It's why I have dogs now. Because he was so wonderful. Followed me around wherever I went."

"I always put cheese in your pockets," he said. She looked at him and saw the smirk on his face. He took a quick look at her and laughed. "Come on, it was funny. I was afraid all the time when you were small. Children are so frightening—full of will and no wits whatsoever, nothing to keep them safe and sound. When I think of Penny, my stomach curls up. That's the right way to think of that little girl dying in the well. Not be... eager about it." The car slowed down momentarily as his foot tensed and lifted off the gas pedal.

"Oh, I don't understand this at all!" Grace cried out. "What's so important about it to her? I mean, why this memory? Couldn't she choose something better?"

Her father's arms made long movements as he turned the car into a parking space. "She can't control where the strokes hit."

She knew that and still resented it.

He got out and waited as she came up next to him. "I know. I hate it too.

"But the odd thing is," he said, starting off to a wooded lot in between two houses. "The odd thing is, how can it be a good memory? That's what gets to me about this. All the time I've known her, she's been a good, kind woman. Who is this, then?"

"Maybe she wasn't a good, kind child?" Grace said hesitantly. There were thorny bushes that caught at her ankles, and bugs flying around. She wasn't a fan of bugs.

"Maybe," her father conceded. "God knows that whole thing must have changed all of us, in one way or another. I thought it would be great to find Penny—you know, hero stuff. I tramped around all over." He stopped to gesture vaguely to the left and right. "Snuck behind houses."

They stepped out of the woods to a slight clearing, with a stone shed. It was bigger than Grace thought it would be. And prettier. There were boards nailed across the door; no one could get in, she was sure. There was a sign as well—Danger! Hazardous! Keep out!

"Why didn't they tear it down?" she asked.

"Historical. Original to a property in the 1700s. Though the door isn't." He pointed. "Just stuck in legal limbo, I guess. Tearing it down was the sentimental choice. But the historical society won a court order and made it safe. And they bought the property. Used to be part of a back yard"—he pointed to the left—"but the owner was glad to get rid of this piece. I imagine someday someone will do something with it, but in the meantime." He shrugged. "In the meantime, it's all your mother cares about."

☙ ☙ ☙

"WHAT DID YOU DO when Penny went missing?" Grace asked her mother.

Her mother leaned forward in a conspiratorial manner. "It was wonderful," she whispered. "All the kids ran around looking for her, meeting up and running off and coming back. In the daytime. At night they don't want any kids on the street."

Grace stiffened as the tense changed, but she said nothing.

"People come out and watch us during the daytime—look up and down, stand with their arms crossed on the porches, or the dads walk up and down their driveways. The police cars come and go. It's so exciting." Her eyes closed and opened again. "Some of the adults thought she'd been kidnapped. Ransom!" she rocked back slightly. "How much do you think it will be? A million dollars was a lot of money then, an amazing amount, so we thought a million dollars or so."

Her mother's eyes were luminous; her lips trembled; it had taken a huge effort to get it all said. She looked out the back window, as if hoping to see something there.

"For a few days, no one got punished for anything they did." She sighed with pleasure.

"But a little girl was dying."

Her mother nodded. "She was. It's true. We knew she was dead before they told us—all at once the whole street changed. The adults walked differently and one by one we knew it was all over. There would never be anything like it again. It was exciting—anything could happen. Maybe a rich woman took her to raise her as her own. Maybe she ran away to the circus; maybe the circus came and got her. I would like the circus." Again she looked out the window. Her eyes welled up and brightened. She looked like she was in love, Grace thought, and then she banished the thought.

"Riding the horses," her mother said. "The trapeze!"

"Mom," she said, "do you know how old you are now?"

Her mother stiffened and her eyes snapped back. "What kind of game is this, Grace?"

"How old am I?"

Her mother took a long look at her, a slow, calculating look. "I'm all right," she said in a whisper. "Penny."

Had she really said *Penny*? Grace sat there frozen, telling herself she was jumping the gun, getting ahead of her mother's illness. Her mother's gaze had fallen again on the diorama, now completed, and she ran her poor hand around the well house, circling it slowly. Grace wanted to slap it aside. She went in search of her father, who sat in the living room with a beer and the TV blaring.

"She's crazy," Grace said flatly.

He turned his head away from her and back to the TV. "But crazy in a stable way," he said. "I have been told."

"What are we going to do?" she cried out, and it was this cry that got her father to sit up suddenly, animated.

"Oh, honey," he said gently, "there's not a damn thing we can do now. It's already happened."

❊ ❊ ❊

THE WEEKS WENT BY rhythmically, Grace thought; she saw her mother, crept home and hid in her skin for a few days, began to think about visiting her mother again, told herself she would accept her mother as she now was—and couldn't. She revolted against it; she wanted to reach some version of the mother she had known, even as she recognized that she couldn't. There were times of course when it seemed she was almost there again, times when she looked at Grace with a glance of deep recognition; but these were brief. Sometimes Grace felt her mother even *chose* to be the way she was now; that she could have fought harder to be her true self again. Her true self. Grace could see her own craziness there. As if this, too, wasn't true.

It was getting hot. Penny had disappeared in late August, and Grace's mother turned her face up to the sun. She began to gather stones, small ones, clutching them one at a time to her waist and dragging herself to a corner in the back yard, where she placed the stones carefully in a rectangle. The shape wavered a little at its corners, and Grace and her father straightened the corners out. Whenever her mother successfully placed a stone she smiled the way a child would smile, without guile and without ambition.

It was hard to watch the effort it took for her mother to find a stone, bend down, pick it up, clutch it, carry it and place it, so Grace and her father began to carry rocks to the well house, stacking them neatly to hurry the thing along. They hadn't even discussed the wisdom of doing it. There was no wisdom anymore. This was just what she wanted, and what they would do.

Grace was shopping for herself one day when she came across a toy store and went in. She found wonderful dolls in there, of all sizes. There were crying baby dolls, and miniature dolls and dolls that stood tall on their own, dolls the size of a 4-year-old girl. That was how old Penny had been when she disappeared. Grace looked at the doll thoughtfully. It would fit inside the well house, and it was the right size.

Then she realized what she was doing, and a paralyzing heat swept through her stomach and up to her head. She waited to catch her breath again, then left the store and went home. She didn't visit her mother again for a week, but then she went there, and found a stone, and placed it on the walls of the well house, which was now as high as her mother's heart.

Her mother began to search for Penny. She opened doors and called her name She crept around the yard, and looked behind the trees. Grace took her for a haircut and a manicure as a treat, and her mother pointed at a small child and cried out, "Penny!" The child turned at the sound and hesitated, and then was pulled away.

But something about that turning, that response, clicked in Grace's mother's brain. She knew Penny was around, now. She had seen her. Penny was on her way to the well.

Her mother fell and broke her good arm, and either the fall or what had caused the fall reduced her mother further. She spent her days on the porch, looking out to the well. She couldn't carry any stones now in either arm. She tried to, bending down and scrabbling in the grass with her right hand, which had lost all flexibility, but she was unable to reach far enough with the cast on her other arm. She stood up, weeping, wandering around in a circle. Her face collapsed. "Woo-woo," she said, and the words came out anguished and weird, like an animal sound, a desperate cry. Grace couldn't bear it; her father came to her mother and bent over, holding her awkwardly.

Grace went back to the store and bought the doll and put it in the back yard, standing it up to face the well house.

Her mother, sitting on the porch, leaned forward eagerly, her eyes on Penny, her face mobile and intelligent.

Sometimes Grace moved Penny closer to the well house, sometimes farther away. Her mother was never in peace if the doll didn't move. Her face broke apart like a two-year-old child's, all incoherent suffering. And they knew how to fix it, how to get her sobs to stop and have that brightness replace the shadow. That's how Grace and her father thought of it: brightness replacing shadow. It was no longer a thing to fight against or judge. Grace's mother required it, this terrible scenery from her childhood. Deny it and she was reduced to a weird high wail. It was only a step from the diorama Grace had been building with her mother, after all. It was merely a memory being drawn from her mother's brain and placed upon the earth again.

And so, they decided to let it be.

Thus day by day Penny froze in position on her way to the well, and each day Grace's mother watched Penny eagerly and anxiously, sometimes stumbling towards her in the yard and veering away at the last moment, her hands bunched, her feet uncertain, a longing on her face that never made it into words. And each time they passed the window, Grace and her father looked out, too, eyes turned to catch a glimpse of Penny, who never reached the well.

Or at least she hadn't, yet.

There was a certainty in all of them that eventually the well would be reached and the long-lost, beloved child would be lost; it was fated to be so. Penny would disappear again, as would Grace's mother. Their lives would submit, briefly, to the compelling absence—submit, pause monumentally, and then go on, as life had done when Penny was first lost, after the sounds had gone and the sorrow faded—as all sounds would go, and all sorrows fade.

# 2

# BALL LIGHTNING

MY UNCLE AL WAS hit by ball lightning while watching his TV, which was near a window. The relatives said it wasn't the window that brought the lightning, but the fact that Uncle Al had put foil on the rabbit ears on his TV set to improve the reception. He was watching the Ed Sullivan show, and while Senor Wences was doing his act, the TV gave a little pop and a bright flash, and a ball of light swept out of the screen and ran straight across the room. Uncle Al said it came to the mirror, smashed it, and made a turn to the right before slamming into a wall and turning it black. He heard thunder as it whacked him on the side of the head—but he didn't know if it was the thunder from outside or whether it was a noise from his own interior turmoil.

My aunts visited him in the hospital and they were suspicious. "Were you drinking?" Aunt Etta asked. "You're always drinking. Could it be it was an alcoholic stroke or something?"

"Go look at my TV," Unle Al said. His head was completely bald and he kept touching it.

"It will grow back," Aunt Louise said. "Why did they shave it?"

"They didn't shave it. It got burned or something, it all fell out. They hooked me up to electrodes to see if there was any brain damage."

The aunts waited.

"I have the brain of a 19-year-old," he said.

The aunts went to Uncle Al's apartment, and indeed, the place was burned black in a line from the TV to the back wall and then in a V to the side wall. They looked at the chair Uncle Al sat in, and it had burned to a crisp. How come Uncle Al was still alive?

"I had just gotten up for a beer," he said, "I don't like Senor Wences that much. Besides, it was raining so hard just then that I wanted to check the windows were shut. I just got up. I was right by the mirror, I saw it coming straight at me. It just hit my ear. They say it's a miracle."

"I understand ball lightning isn't as strong as regular lightning," Aunt Etta said, pursing her lips. "Now if *real* lightning had hit your apartment, I don't think there'd be anything left. If *real* lightning had hit you on your ear, I think your head would explode."

Uncle Al glared at her. "My hair exploded," he said angrly. "Every hair on my head exploded. Isn't that enough?"

"You were losing it anyway, how much was really left?"

Uncle Al and Aunt Etta had always had a testy relationship. Uncle Al got the big bedroom, because he was a boy. Aunt Etta and Aunt Louise had to share a room, because they were girls. My mother had her own little room behind the kitchen, because she was the youngest by ten years. She was babied and petted and never part of the sibling rivalry.

"I can't believe you're jealous that I got hit by lightning and you didn't," he finally said.

"You *didn't* get hit by lightning," she huffed. "Just your ear. The ear is hardly even a part of your body. Not even skin and bones, just cartilage."

"Lean over," he said, "let me cut your ear off and see if it's a part of your body."

Aunt Etta didn't lean over; but she wasn't about to let her brother stay in the center of attention. In the next year, she traveled to Florida, Ohio, California and Maine. She went to the Museum of String, the Crystal Caves, the World's Biggest Quarry, and the Last of the Sequoias. She drew up a list of all the people she'd met, and where they'd come from originally. She had it laminated.

On the first Sunday after Christmas, the whole family always got together and showed slides of important points in the past year. Aunt Etta had boxes of pictures; she showed herself sitting on a big rock, standing under a big tree, staring over a quarry ledge, and standing at the start of a string labyrinth.

Uncle Al showed the slide of his room after the lightning struck, and the headlines of a local paper, "Rare ball lightning attacks local man." Then there was a TV documentary on strange but true cases, and they interviewed Uncle Al and his doctors. He got a reel from the producers and showed it as a home movie on the projection screen. Soon after that, Aunt Etta said she was thinking of moving to Washington state. She said no one ever talked about lightning over there, it was a matter of small interest and even less use.

My uncle Al was tone deaf until he was struck by ball lightning. When it happened, he was knocked off his chair and lay on the floor. His ears were ringing. He was seeing lots of blue around him—boxes of blue hung in the air. He shut his eyes and the boxes became purple.

Uncle Al was single, but he had good neighbors in his building. Of course, most people were home watching Ed Sullivan, and in fact, the ball lightning had shorted out all the wiring in the building. The people below him heard a crash, the lights went out, and they took their flashlights and ran upstairs to bang on the outside of his door.

Uncle Al crawled to the door and let them in. They thought he'd been robbed, at first. Uncle Al kept shaking his head slowly—he suddenly couldn't hear anything—but then they noticed the TV, which had burst outwards and was still smoking.

They sent a kid to run down the street and call an ambulance.

Uncle Al was deaf for three weeks. Then, when his hearing cleared, he heard noises all the time. At first they bothered him, but then he realized something.

"They're *notes*," he told Aunt Louise, who liked to listen to show tunes. "I think I'm hearing scales of notes. Didn't you used to play scales when you took piano lessons?"

"Sure," Aunt Louise said. "Everyone has to play scales. Like this." And she hummed some Chopsticks for Uncle Al.

He shook his head. "No. Not that." He listened for a while and then he hummed what he was hearing.

"That's a scale," Aunt Louise said. "I think it's a minor scale, but really, I only took four lessons. At any rate, it sounds good to me."

Uncle Al went to music teachers then so he could learn to play what he heard in his head. Mostly, no one wanted to see him more than once, because he couldn't play anything except what he heard—the notes in his head confused him if he tried to practice anything else. So the teachers became formal and disinterested. Except for Miss Gutcheon. She asked him to hum things, and then she wrote them down. And then she held his hands over the keys and made him repeat it. She taught him all the scales, and then she would call out a key to him and he would hum it. And then she wrote little duets based on what he heard. "You have perfect pitch," she said. "It's a rare thing. Of course you have to learn what the notes are called first, before you can sing them. But you're perfect once you do."

Uncle Al was amazed. "I never had it before," he said. "Couldn't hold a tune at all. People told me to shut up—at least my family did."

Miss Gutcheon smiled. "But you sound beautiful now. I love to hear you." She blushed.

Uncle Al told his sisters what Miss Gutcheon said, and Aunt Etta looked at him thoughtfully. "Perfect pitch? I've heard of it." She thought for a moment. "But what good is it?"

Uncle Al was a machinist for the subways. He usually had oil on his hands (maybe that was why the ball lightning went for him?). He had never been interested in music, didn't much listen to the radio, liked funny songs rather than good ones, and had no idea what the point of perfect pitch was. But he had it, and he was proud of it. He went to Miss Gutcheon's recitals for children and adults, and he could tell when they played a wrong note. He knew what her range was: her laughter was in C, her disappointments in A, she soothed children in B-flat. His sister began to suspect he was in love.

And then one day he lost it. First his hearing had gone, and then it had come back in a wonderful way. And then the wonderful way cleared up as well. No more scales, no familiar pitches. When he heard music, it just sounded nice or annoying, not recognizable.

It was devastating. Miss Gutcheon was sympathetic, but without that one thing about him, Uncle Al didn't seem all that exciting anymore. She was delicate about saying it, came up with pretty excuses not to see him, and little disappearances out of town, but Uncle Al knew enough to stop going to her recitals, and she took back the recording of medieval chants (pure human notes! she had once cried out) she had lent him.

So life went back to what it was. His sisters chipped in and got him a really good television, one that didn't need tinfoil to pick up the signals. He never saw Miss Gutcheon again, as far as I knew, and that didn't satisfy me. I would race down the block when I knew a storm was coming, and stand across the street, watching his window. When the thunder cracked and the sky got dark, I would see him open the window and lean out. Sometimes he'd hold out his hand. I found this unbearable, and beautiful, and I'd imagine that someday I too would be broken by a strike of love. I couldn't leave it that way, however, so I took the wires I found from discarded lamps on the street, or useless toasters—any electrical appliance—and I made long, thin, uninsulated strands that I brought with me when I went to visit him.

When he went to the bathroom or to the kitchen, I'd sneak my newest wires out and attach them to the wires I'd already laid around his apartment. One line ran from the phone jack; another from his doorbell. One came from his floor lamp, another from the new TV's grounding wire. All the lines ran toward the window, where they met in a single wrapped strand that I snaked out the window sill and then separated outside. There I extended them, pressing them into the ribs of the brick exterior, splaying out. I was careful to observe from across the street whether anything showed, but nothing did.

By winter I had constructed a kind of spider web around his window: wires wrapped around wires, thin filaments designed to give back to Uncle Al what he had once had: Magic. Love. Life.

Nothing ever happened. One or two of the wires were removed—I imagine one of the aunts found them and discarded them silently, quick to assume it was a clue to her brother's mania.

I thought, for many years, that I had done him an immense favor, by trying to trick him back into the life he loved. It wasn't until I myself was old, and knew that love wasn't always magic, that I realized he must have known about some of it at least. He wasn't unobservant. And I know, too, that until he died he went to the window whenever there was a storm, and looked at the sky, and placed one hand firmly on the wires I had run through the window frame. He would have known that a second strike could kill him, even if I didn't know it. But he let the wire reach his skin, let the chances arrange themselves in the thickening air, because even though he wasn't strong enough to act, he was strong enough to believe. And he believed for the rest of his life, alone.

# 3

# MOTHER IS SLIPPING

I WAS SHOCKED WHEN MY mother said that Helen Anders got what she deserved, nosey snooping hag. Helen Anders had fallen down the stairwell the previous month, broken her hip, finally dying of pneumonia. My mother hinted she'd been pushed, raised her eyebrows, and grinned.

Until recently, my mother never said unjust things about people, much less hinted at murder, and I wasn't totally used to it yet. My mother glanced my way, catching the surprise. A shadow flickered over her face and something fled behind her eyes and then she said, "Colder than it should be today. Well, soon we'll be complaining about the heat." She grinned at her wisdom. She was back to normal, and nattered on about the weather and the TV shows (which she couldn't remember but always watched).

I replayed the scene on the way home. I had definitely heard it. "It was so odd," I said to Vic that night.

"Oh well, people complain," my husband said. He was medium-sized and clearly balding, which he accepted patiently. He saw patient acceptance as the trick to life. I do not; if I had to declare myself I would say life took constant effort. Patience was too passive, despite the fact that Vic seemed to do all right with it. It was partially this god of his, patience, that persuaded him to try to balance whatever I said. In fact, my mother did that too, in a way, always taking the opposite of my point of view, just to point out how other people saw things. I hated it from either one and would try to store my thoughts for some other time, so as not to get distracted. He glanced up at me as I went about, moving things here and there. When I'm upset, I walk around the living room. When he's upset ... well, he never is. "Does it sound like something she'd do, really?" he asked, his eyebrows up.

"No. Of course not. I don't think. But it doesn't sound like something she'd *say*, either."

He shook his head. "You don't give yourself enough credit. You get surprised and you think right away that you must have been wrong for a long time. Maybe there's something else going on."

Like what? But that's the way he handles things; always trying to negotiate a fair settlement.

✥ ✥ ✥

My mother has always been brightly superficial, a bit of a chatterbox, going on and on about nothing, seemingly incapable of noticing how boring it is to talk about weather, TV, items in the newspaper. What else is there to talk about? Oh yes, the meaning of life and love. My mother has never once spoken about life and love.

But Vic's suggestion stuck in my mind and the next couple of visits I simply put some questions about recent events and then events a few months ago, and then a year ago; I even asked her about her favorite TV program. "What are you talking about?" she said at one point. "You're making things up. There's never been a show like that."

But two months later, the show returned on reruns and when I asked, she said, "My favorite show. I always liked it." She settled back with pleasure. "That boy on it with the curly hair—I think he's gonna win."

"You mean the moderator? Bill?" I gave her a chance to notice he was a moderator, not a contestant.

"That's the one."

The odd conversations were gradually accumulating. Were they strange or only just a little off? My mother always considered herself to be a character; maybe this was deliberate. I called her sister, my Aunt Lou, in Delaware and said I thought mom was acting strange.

"Seems fine to me," Aunt Lou said. "Of course she forgets things, she's over 80."

"I know that," I said. People who tell you the obvious always put me off. "She talks so much you think she knows what she's talking about. Next time, ask her some questions about what you did the last time you saw her."

"I don't even remember that," Aunt Lou said. She laughed; she was seventy.

❈ ❈ ❈

I HAD TO CONSIDER whether mom had killed someone—although this raised the question of whether she was actually smart enough to kill someone, though she had indeed been smarter when she was younger. And what did smartness have to do with it anyway? I don't know how smart jellyfish are, and they kill. Just about every animal kills; for food, mostly, but for territory as well. So the animal part of mom might indeed be a killer.

Though she wasn't purely the animal part, of course. Her eyes could look knowing as she said something that made my teeth grate; but then she'd say the opposite of what she said before, and animals don't contradict themselves. She'd say she would never have said what she said before, it wasn't like her. I didn't think she really has ever been aware of what's "like her." That made me wonder if I'm aware of what's "like me."

Nevertheless.

My mother's neighbor fell down the stairs and died, eventually. And my mother gloated over it. That's what I decided to settle on.

Mom had developed a hatred for Helen, though my mother would insist that she is not the kind of person who hates people—and really, she never was. She was pleasant and friendly, a little coy, a little jesting. "Helen's a nasty woman; and that's not hatred. It's just the truth," she said. Was this kind of statement any different from hate?

My mother was not the kind of person who believed in strict truth, anyway: she said what she thought people hoped to hear. Do I do that?

Late last year, mom started complaining that someone was taking her things or moving her things. She was getting forgetful; she spent the next few months sorting her drawers, labeling folders for her filing cabinet, placing her dishes on little wire shelves so she could see them more easily and thus could count them quickly. Aunt Lou called it inventorying. Mom had retired a long time ago, she was having trouble getting around; she had too much time on her hands. When they were young, Aunt Lou said, my mother was the restless one. But mom was 12 years older than Aunt Lou; it might have been just how it looked to a little girl watching a teenager. I tried to accept Aunt Lou's view of things: I wished she could come and see for herself more often, but her husband was going through cancer treatment; there was no emergency.

The inventorying kept mom busy for a few months, but then she said that someone was breaking in and taking her money.

She always kept her money in the underwear drawer; it was probably where all thieves looked for money.

When she started complaining about theft, I was concerned. Aunt Lou said, no, she was just getting forgetful. Aunt Lou had once found her own money in the utensils drawer. "Hasn't that ever happened to you?"

she asked. "You get distracted, you're on the phone or whatever, and you don't notice what you're doing."

"Well," I'd said. "She does get easily distracted."

"Trust me," Aunt Lou said. "She's moving the money herself and forgetting it. That's the only good thing about getting old," she sighed. "People have to start making allowances. Give her a break. She's doing fine. Don't jump on everything she does."

But then mom told she me she'd found out who was stealing her money. It was her neighbor, Helen. She'd woken up one night and Helen was standing by her bedside, staring at her. Helen put her finger to her lips, opened the underwear drawer, and took half of mom's money.

"Why would she do that?" I interrupted. "Only half?" None of it made sense to me, so I was glomming onto details.

"She's going to come back for the other half," my mother said. She was angry. "I can't let her take my money. The nerve of her!"

"This is so strange," I said. My mind was spinning. "Do you want me to talk to her?"

"Could you?" my mother said, relieved. "Tell her to stop doing it. I don't like it at all. Doesn't she have her own money?"

"Well, maybe that's it," I answered feebly. "Maybe she's broke?"

My mother shook her head. "Not her," she said dismissively. "She wears a new fur coat every day. She keeps the heads on them, too! Not just the fox stoles, but she's got raccoon heads and bear heads on them. It's disgusting."

I'd never seen her wear a fur; she wore cloth coats or a cheap bubble coat in the winter. I told myself to slow down, think it over carefully, let everything fall into place bit by bit.

"Helen used to be all right, didn't she? Didn't she always say hello and ask if you wanted her newspaper?"

"That was *my* newspaper. She takes my newspaper too." My mother looked triumphant. Her mouth, I thought, was funny. It twisted a little; it had a hard look.

"I'll take care of it," I said. "Have you been to the store lately? Should we take a trip to the supermarket?" I couldn't stand the conversation any more; I couldn't believe what she was saying about Helen, a very small, quiet old lady who'd always seemed friendly enough. My mother went to get her grocery list, and the topic was done for the day.

❊ ❊ ❊

"I REALLY DO THINK there's something wrong with mom," I told Aunt Lou.

"You always think that." she sighed. "Look, you expect too much. She's old, she lives alone, she's doing all right. She knows enough to call if there's a problem."

"She thinks Helen is breaking in at night and stealing from her."

"Probably just a vivid dream. Things get a little confusing when you're old. We were talking about some of her friends the other day and she said that one of them's dying. It can't be easy; so many of her friends have died." My aunt was so pragmatic, so willing to stay way from implications. On the other hand, was I the one to leap where I should only stride? Her friends were dying; that could have knocked her for a loop. Maybe she felt alone and vulnerable.

"You think she's depressed?" I asked. "She could be depressed. That would explain her lack of focus."

"There you go again. She's old, her friends are dying; can't she feel sad without thinking it's a condition?"

"It's just that she's saying bizarre things. This latest thing about Helen stealing from her—"

"It's harmless. Really."

"I think I should take her to a doctor and have her tested."

My aunt laughed. "Why not? If it will make you feel better. But I talk to her all the time, and I think she's fine."

❊ ❊ ❊

MOM AGREED TO GO to the doctor to have her medications evaluated; I had read how confusion in the elderly was often caused by the combination of medications they were on. In fact, I was convinced this must be true; she had nine pills she took every day. At first she looked brighter when I told her this, and she thought it was a good idea; she'd been getting absent-minded and maybe they could find out why. But as the day got closer, she refused to fill out the forms; she wondered why she needed to go; she flat-out refused. "This is nonsense. Why do I have to go to a new doctor? I like my doctor just fine. Are you trying to say there's something wrong with me? My memory is no worse than anyone else's; do you remember everything? Why are you trying to blame me?" Her eyes got a little glazed; I was terrified she would cry. Was I the kind of daughter who made her mother cry?

"You need to see someone," I said, trying to sound nonjudgmental. "But there's no rush. We'll do it some other time. It's just a checkup, after all. Maybe I should just talk to your doctor?"

I was lying; her doctor was an idiot; I was just trying to get her used to the idea. And me too.

❊ ❊ ❊

A WHILE AGO, A month or two after Helen died, I made some mashed potatoes and brought them to her because she said she longed for mashed potatoes. She has severe arthritis in her hands. I always left the peels in mashed potatoes, and Vic liked them that way, too, but she refused to eat them. "You should peel them first, you know. I've never seen this kind of thing—what is this, garbage scraps? Everyone peels them first." She looked at the potatoes suspiciously.

"It's better if you leave the skins on. Nutritionally," I said.

She looked at me and kept the look going. "I'll throw them out," I said. I got up hastily and dropped the pot in the garbage.

"Wasting food," my mother said. "We never wasted food in my house."

"Please don't criticize me, I was just trying to help."

"Criticize? Criticize? I never criticize. You're just too sensitive. You always want to make me out the bad guy."

"Fine. I apologize." It's the only way I can stop her; it makes her look gratified. "Did Mrs. Ramirez bring your groceries?" Mrs. Ramirez is the downstairs neighbor I hired to come in a few days a week. I had just started doing it; Aunt Lou thought it was ridiculous—mom wouldn't go for it, what was the point, etc. I did it anyway, asking her to stop by twice a week, a few hours each day. She'd been there twice.

"Oh, her. I don't know why you bother. I can get my own."

She sat there, with her four-pronged cane next to the chair, her hands held neatly on her lap.

"Of course you can," I said. "It's just that you've earned the right to relax a little."

"How can I relax? You keep sending people to my house. Do you think that's relaxing?"

"They're just to help you. Don't they help you? And wait—what do you mean by 'people'? It's just Mrs. Ramirez."

"Then why does Johnny keep coming by asking for money to pay them?"

We sat in silence for a moment. Her eyes darted around a little, then they settled on the hands in her lap. I could see her assembling something to say.

"When did he come?" I asked, before she had time to change the subject.

She looked cagey now, and a little frightened. "What did I say?" she asked. "Did I say something wrong? I can't remember what I said."

"You said Johnny wants money."

"Did I say Johnny?" she asked, moving back to relax in her chair. "I meant Paul, the guy who gets me the paper. He's an excellent, excellent neighbor," she said, smiling with her teeth showing.

❀ ❀ ❀

Mother laughs; she laughs about nothing, she laughs when she thinks someone else has been foolish. She doesn't see herself as foolish. Her laugh, which I've heard mocking people all my life—her laugh sometimes stops me dead, when I'm thinking of what I did during the day; I can see her bright eyes watching me as she laughs: Look at what she did!

She often rocks back and forth, laughing, all by herself, because she thinks she's witty, though she can't remember the right words now. But it doesn't matter, she's got the rhythm of the thing down pat.

I really must do better at it. I really must be a nicer person. I could pick up flowers, cakes, magazines or those fake cards with their fake cheer that she hoards as if they were wishes granted to her that she has yet to cash in. I must be her evil stepdaughter; she must be the fairy godmother.

"Where did you put that paper I had?" she asked me.

"What paper?"

"I had it right here." She shuffled things around on her table. She had, by my count, five piles of papers. She started with one, then sorted it, and then she forgot what the sorting meant, so she started over. Her face was getting tighter. She looked at me suspiciously. "I know you have it," she said.

"I don't."

"You could be nice, once in a while," she said, taking a new tack.

"Apparently not," I muttered.

"Do you hate me?" she asked, and her voice was broken, and I hung my head.

"No. You're mistaken," I whispered. "I never said that."

She looked uncertain. "No?"

"No."

She looked away. Her intelligence comes and goes, and I can't tell when it will be there, or if it's always there and she just gets tired and bears with it all, for the moment indifferent.

I bent down to kiss her cheek, and left.

It should be easier to be kind.

❈ ❈ ❈

THE NEXT TIME I visited, my mother was crying. I could see wads of tissues. Her eyes looked red; but she denied it.

"It's the pollen," she said, sniffing. "Always had a problem with pollen."

"It's February."

She nodded. "That's when it starts."

"Well," I said. "And what have you been up to?"

There was a hesitation, a bit of a sigh, then she pasted a bright look on her face. Her eyes still had a shine from the tears. "I called Margie," she said. "You remember her? We used to work together. To see how she was. You know, she can hardly walk these days. Her daughter takes care of her, drives her wherever she wants to go, takes her to the movies if she wants, or the doctor. What a thing, huh? I really think that's terrific. I envy those women who live with their daughters." Her smile at the end became genuine; she snuck a little look at me, not directly, just out of the corner of her eyes, to see how I was taking it.

"Yes, well, those daughters have no life," I said quickly.

"Oh I'm sure they do." Her mouth got tight; I'm sure my mouth got tight as well.

"No, they don't. You know that would never work, we'd be on each other's nerves all day."

"I'll be good. We'll both be good. You could move in here, with me, or I could stay with you. I'd rather you moved in here. After all, I'm the one who's getting older. I probably have more things I'm attached to."

"I'm attached to my things! My husband is too!" I said sharply, then I heard myself. Talking about things! How did we get there? "Mom, it's not a question of who can move where; it's not going to happen. I'm sorry, but I'm not going to make believe this would work out."

"You're so hard," she said. A tear ran down her face—a real tear; I knew a heartfelt tear.

"I'm sorry." I stuck my hand out and took her hand. "We're just not the kinds of people who can live together. We'd be on each other all day long, and how would that feel?"

"Can't you be a little in control of yourself?" she asked. "Just to be nice to your mother a little bit more?"

"I'm here almost every day." I was starting to bristle.

"For five minutes. You rush right off."

"I'm here for two hours, usually. When I have appointments, and I can't stay, then I leave."

"I'm not complaining."

"You *are* complaining."

"Oh, please, can't you take a joke? I was just kidding."

"Where was the joke, mom? I don't get it."

She was exasperated, once again. And once again, we were going round and round without actually knowing what, exactly, was the issue. How many daughters visited their mothers so often? Took them to doctors, supermarkets? All right, how many always got into some kind of bad feeling or argument? It was a hard role to play.

We sank into a funk. My mother rallied first and said, "Johnny came over with his girlfriend, did I tell you?"

I felt the time slacken, just a little. "Did he," I said flatly, and my mother shut her mouth and rose to go make tea.

❦ ❦ ❦

I CALLED AUNT LOU. "Mom says Johnny's back."

I heard my aunt's sharp intake of air. "He's out of jail?"

"She says he comes by for money."

A beat or two of silence. "But maybe she's imagining it?" It was the first time Aunt Lou admitted that mom might be making anything up.

"I don't remember when he was due to come up for parole. Do you?"

"No. I don't think about him if I don't have to."

"One of us should find out."

Silence.

"I'm dealing with mom," I said finally. "You find out." I didn't think I had the nerve to discover he was truly back.

❦ ❦ ❦

JOHNNY IS MY BROTHER. He's a pyromaniac. I suppose there's something in the gene pool—mother might have killed her neighbor or I'm a suspicious bitch, and Johnny destroys things. All of them different kinds of destruction. As for Aunt Lou, she keeps her distance and maybe that keeps her safe.

Johnny set small fires as a child. My parents smelled smoke one day when he was five, and found a fire in a waste basket. They smacked his hand and took away the matches, and rightly blamed themselves for leaving matches around. My father smoked, and my mother swore that was the reason Johnny was fascinated with smoke and fire. She nagged my father to quit—or at least, as things turned out, to *say* he'd quit, because though he never smoked in the house again, he went out often for walks or to meet the guys in the local bar, and every time he came back smelling of cigarettes.

When he turned twelve, Johnny started fires out in the yard or in abandoned lots or behind stores in the garbage bins. He was caught many times, and eventually, when something valuable burned up, he began to have a juvenile record. My parents kept strict rules—straight to school and straight back.

He set a fire in the schoolyard and got expelled. My parents tried to argue that he should have been supervised, it was a small fire, there was no harm done, but that was it. He was sent to a military school, where for two years he had no reports against him, until he burned his own bed. My parents checked him into a boarding school for troubled children, where he stayed until he was 18 and then left.

He came home, had dinner with us, and in the middle of the night doused the front of the house with gasoline and burned the house down. We got out through the rear door. He was arrested and sent to prison, released four or five years later, and for a while things were quiet. Then one day our new home caught on fire—no accelerant this time, but we didn't need a message from him.

We moved without giving anyone our forwarding address, to a new state. Aunt Lou moved to Delaware, I went off to college, we all settled down alertly, and my parents moved from place to place whenever they smelled smoke, or thought they smelled smoke. I moved once, too, when there was a fire two streets away from where I lived, but that was probably just coincidence.

After my father died of heart failure, my mother moved into a co-op community with a front desk, where Johnny's picture was blown up with red warning notes around it.

And then it was quiet for a long time.

I suspected Johnny had become an arsonist for hire. What else would he do? His early attempts were clumsy, but he loved his work; after he got out of prison the first time he was free for a while and didn't find us. But we were notified a few years later, about a bigger trial, and we called to find out that he was convicted and got a longer sentence. We breathed easily for a very long time, somewhat conscious that he could get out on parole—what did we know? It was always better not to know, always better not to call the detectives or court officers to track him. We didn't want him to catch our scent. So we kept slips of paper with the numbers we could call if we wanted to find out where he was, but it was always best not to.

When I married I felt a little safer, or at least not alone when I smelled something odd just before I went to bed; I could ask Vic if he noticed anything, now, and that was a relief.

And then, ten years without a word or a hint. Still in jail? Maybe even dead. It was not a nice thing to wish about a brother, certainly.

❈ ❈ ❈

MY AUNT PROMISED TO see if she could find out where Johnny was.

Less than a week later, my mother called me at six in the morning, sobbing, "There's something wrong! Come over right away. There's something wrong with me!" Her voice was terrified; it woke me up immediately.

"Should I call the ambulance?"

"No, just come over. I'll wait until you come over."

"What is it?" Vic asked, and I told him. He dressed as fast as I did, and drove me over there.

We rushed in to find mom in the living room, watching TV. She turned it off, looking at me in amazement. "What are you doing here?" she said. "You should have called."

"Mom. You called *me*. You said something was wrong. You said to get here right away. I almost called the ambulance."

Her face, which had been amazed, now started to shut down. "I never called. I think you've made a mistake. I would remember if I called."

"I heard the phone, Millie," Vic said.

Mom took a moment to think. "You heard the phone, but you didn't hear me?" she said finally, her chin raised.

I took the time while they were talking to get my bearings back. I still needed to know if something was wrong. "Do you feel all right?" I asked.

"Well, I've gotten old," she said slyly.

Vic looked at his watch. "Is it okay if I leave you here? I've got to get to work."

"Fine," I said. "I'll take the bus."

"All this fuss for nothing," mom said evenly.

She called again two nights later, after midnight. When we got there, she was asleep.

When she called the third time, I told her to call me back in fifteen minutes; she didn't.

❉ ❉ ❉

"MOM'S LOSING IT," I told my aunt. "She keeps calling and there's nothing wrong."

"Oh, that," she said. "She's called me a few times, too. I talked to her about it. She just feels lonely. I tell her to turn the TV on."

"Really? She told me to come right over, there was something wrong. The last time was in the middle of the night."

"She's okay," Aunt Lou said. "Just talk to her for a bit; talk her out of it. Don't get so dramatic. She's old and she just got frightened for a minute. Get her to think of something else."

What do you do when no one sees what you're seeing? How do you convince them? Or do you finally accept what they say? Aunt Lou and mom were close; they had always relied on each other; when there was a crisis of any kind, they sought each other out. If Aunt Lou thought mom was doing all right; if she knew what was going on and dismissed my worries—who was right?

❊ ❊ ❊

AUNT LOU SAID JOHNNY was still in jail; she had checked with a probation officer he'd had years before; this officer had checked the system.

"You see?" I said. "There's something wrong. She says she saw Johnny, she's making these calls. I'm still getting them. When I told her to turn on the TV, she called me a lousy daughter and hung up the phone. I called her back ten minutes later; she didn't answer. So I went there."

"And she was fine."

"And she was fine. She said she didn't know what I was talking about. She always says that I'm making things up."

"Just go along with it."

"Then what about Johnny?"

"Well, he's in prison, so that's all right."

"But she said she saw him."

"She didn't," my aunt said firmly. "So there's nothing to worry about."

❊ ❊ ❊

WE CARRY OURSELVES AS children around with us, like a twin who never grows. Is my mother sometimes the child she was, with the sound of her mother's objections in her head? I remember her mother as mostly silent; I suspect I will be silent, that maybe it alternates in generations: the ones who withdraw, the ones who do battle.

I didn't have children. I think that's a good thing.

Mother fell in the street; was she clipped by a car or she just got surprised by it, not seeing it as she began to cross. And that driver—he didn't see her or didn't care? Maybe she was in his blind spot.

She lay in the street until people came running forward, asking what hurt, calling police, ambulances. She got up; she refused all aid.

She called me the next day. "If you came here more often, you'd know what I'm going through. I don't know what's happening to me. I get confused," she said. She sounded old and hurt. I went over, and she sat there with her bruised face, watching me avidly, hungrily, until it got on my nerves. "Why are you staring at me?" I asked.

"I'm not staring," she said. "Can't I look?"

❊ ❊ ❊

MY HUSBAND TRIES TO support me, but he can't figure out which angle to take. He's pointed out that my mother is old and failing—as if I were too dumb to figure it out myself. He's said she's always been difficult—as if that makes this any easier. There's no answer he can give that will make his side of the conversation acceptable. He knows that now. He's getting good at being guarded. He rubs my shoulder or my back and asks if I want a cup of coffee.

❊ ❊ ❊

AFTER THE CAR ACCIDENT, I insisted on an aide until my mother felt better. She was taking pain pills and they must have made her groggy, because she agreed. Then she called my aunt to complain that the aide was stealing from her.

"She isn't stealing," I told Aunt Lou. "Mom is getting paranoid. Besides, what is there to steal?"

"Well, I can see she won't get much love from you on this point."

"Aunt Lou, she's confused. Her memory's shot. She's getting worse. We should do something."

"We are doing something. You've got that aide there, after all. She hates the aide, and I think you should consider that maybe the aide *is* stealing something. Just consider it. As a courtesy."

"As a *courtesy*, I should think someone's a thief?"

"See? You go too far. I want you to respect her feelings, and you make it into something crazy."

"*I'm* not crazy," I said angrily. "Mom's crazy. She's the one we're talking about, remember?"

"Why do you have to be so difficult," my aunt murmured. "Listen, I know what you're saying, but she's doing all right. She's holding on. And I don't want to upset her any more than she is upset. So maybe this aide isn't the right aide. I mean, if she thinks this aide is stealing, what does it matter if she is or not? Let's just get a new aide."

"It's somebody's livelihood," I said weakly.

"It's your mother," my aunt answered, and won.

❖ ❖ ❖

THE NEXT AIDE HAD a thick accent; my mother couldn't understand her, and neither could I. She tried to do all the chores I left on a list taped to the door, until my mother took all the clothes out of the washer and dumped them on the floor, stating that the aide was poisoning the clothes.

"She used a strange detergent," my aunt said. "I saw the box. It has a foreign symbol on it." My aunt had driven down recently to visit.

"You make it sound so reasonable."

"You make too much of it."

"I think she has Alzheimer's," I blurted suddenly.

Aunt Lou was silent for a moment. "I don't care what she has, she needs to be treated the right way. I promised her years ago that she could die in her own apartment. That's what she wants, you know, to die in her own place, in her own time. I made that promise and I'm going to keep it."

"How?" I asked. "She can't live alone much longer, and she fights the aides. She fights everything I do."

"Well, then, maybe you're doing the wrong thing."

❈ ❈ ❈

SINCE HELEN WAS DEAD, it was now the aide who came into her room at night, stealing her money. This was the new aide, who had a different accent, whose name my mother couldn't pronounce. This one was nasty, my mother said, always glaring at her and cursing in a made-up language. My mother bolted the door from the inside, so I took down the bolt.

"That aide is worse than the other one," my aunt said. "Besides, Millie doesn't want an aide. It's just upsetting her."

"Aunt Lou, she has to get used to it. She can't live alone much longer. Either she moves to a home or she gets aides."

"This will just make her crazier sooner. It's not good for her."

"So what's your suggestion?"

"Find someone she likes."

But there was no one she liked, and I said that to my mother.

"I like everyone!" she protested. "This person, whatever her name is, why is she here? I can manage. I've always managed. Don't do this to me. I'll ask Johnny if I can move in with him—"

"Johnny said no. I asked him." My heart pounded a little. I was not used to lying.

Mom regarded me suspiciously. In the next room, the newest aide changed the bed. I had told her my mother was difficult and her lips had gone in a line as she nodded. I wouldn't have to fire this one; she would quit. She had already complained twice that mom had insulted her.

"Why do you want to have someone watching me all the time? What do you get out of it? You just want to order me around, don't you? Because I ordered you around as a child. Some kind of getting even. I don't understand why you didn't grow up kinder. I was always good to you."

"Mom!" She drew in her breath. "I'm trying to help."

"What did I ever do?" my mother moaned. "Why can't you let me live the way I want? I *don't want her here!*" Her voice was raised; she glanced out of the corner of her eyes in the aide's direction

The aide appeared. "Time to go, ma'am," she said, looking at me. "Can't come tomorrow, sorry. Daughter maybe sick."

I understood.

My mother stared stonily away, refusing to see the aide.

"Thank you, Veronica," I said as she left.

"Who's Veronica? Is that her name? She said she was Mary." My mother's shoulders began to relax.

I had asked each aide to say she was Mary; it was the only name my mother could remember.

I ran into mom's neighbor, a young woman with a dog. "Is everything okay with your mother? Do you want me to check her occasionally?"

"What happened?" I asked, already feeling defeated.

"She asked if she could move in with me. She started yelling about thieves one night, in the hallway and I came out to see what was going on. Does she have Alzheimer's or something? My grandmother did."

"I'm so sorry," I said. "Yes. I'm still trying to get her to the doctor. She refuses."

"Trick her," the neighbor said. "So many things can happen to them."

\* \* \*

MOM'S FRIEND, MARGIE, HAD called me the day before. Twice now, Mom had asked to move in with her.

I made an appointment with a neurologist. I filled out all the forms. I told mom we were going to the movies.

When I pulled outside a doctor's office, I said it was my doctor and it would only take a minute. When the nurse came out, I asked if mom would go with me and she smiled. I had a story every step of the way—they wanted to talk to her privately, they needed family history, etc. Because I was the one who was "sick," mom went out of her way to be helpful.

Though some of the things they asked were crazy, she said afterwards. Picking out the thing that didn't fit, remembering numbers.

"Ah well, I think they do surveys on populations. Comparing cognitive abilities from one decade to the next, that kind of thing. They did the same with me."

"I hope they didn't charge you for it," she said.

\* \* \*

SHE DIDN'T REMEMBER THEY'D done a scan of her brain. The technician was terrific, apparently, and said she was in training, would mom minding helping her out?

We didn't get a diagnosis for eight weeks. It was Alzheimer's.

My aunt said, "I knew it."

"Did you? You always seemed to think she was fine."

"Of course not. I just don't want to upset her. It might make it worse."

"It *only* gets worse, Aunt Lou."

"Of course. But not right now. It may be years before she gets really bad."

This was driving me crazy, too, this doggedness to let things ride. How was this possible? How could anyone believe my mother could continue to live alone? I was having trouble with the aides and my aunt thought that they should stop for a while.

"The doctor said she should have someone around her more."

"You said that. Yes. Well, maybe you can try bringing her to a senior center? There's daycare for old people; maybe she'd like that."

"And we'll need a live-in aide, too, right?" I was hopeful; she had never suggested anything before.

❊ ❊ ❊

MY MOTHER HATED THE senior center. She cried or yelled. She locked herself in the bathroom at home once to avoid going to the center, and then, confused, locked herself in the bathroom at the center, thinking she was home.

I took the knobs off the stove and hid them. The aide (there was a new one) could make meals and leave snacks; I told the aide where the knobs were.

Mom called whoever was on speed dial; she couldn't remember our phone numbers. She begged people to come over: her doctor, the handyman, the co-op board, old friends. She asked for help: she said something terrible was happening; she said she was lost; she asked if she could go live with them.

There were probably more things that I didn't know about. I reported everything I knew to Aunt Lou. I wanted to move my mother someplace safe—some facility used to handling Alzheimer's patients. Aunt Lou was mom's health proxy; I wasn't certain enough of myself to try to overrule her.

I got more aides, trying to convince my aunt that mom was adjusting to them, but when my aunt called her, mom was hysterical. Mom began to hang up on me when I called; she cried when I visited.

I let the last aide go without replacing her; I was worn out. I decided to spend the day with mom, just watching, just trying to see if I was exaggerating, as my aunt claimed.

I called mom early and said I would take her to breakfast. I planned a relaxing day: a little shopping, a trip to the park, going over her mail.

As I got near her apartment, I heard sirens and pulled over to let a fire truck pass me by. I slammed on the gas once it passed and roared to my mother's street, getting as close as I could. The street was blocked by emergency vehicles.

❊ ❊ ❊

It wasn't much of a fire. Just the kitchen. A lot of smoke damage. Mom's hands were burned. She had used the pliers to turn a knob on the stove in order to make me pancakes (she thought I was coming over for breakfast). She put oil in the pan and went off to find the pancake mix, stopping to turn on the radio, and then forgot about the pan.

When she smelled smoke she ran into the kitchen. The oil had caught on fire and it terrified her. She couldn't find the pliers, she didn't know what to do, so she turned on the water and began filling cups with water and throwing them at the fire, sloshing the flames around.

Her neighbors called 911.

She didn't answer the door so the firefighters broke in, and by then she was sobbing on the kitchen floor, her hands burned, her face smudged, her eyes wild.

They kept her in the hospital overnight, until her blood pressure stabilized. The social worker at the hospital suggested a nursing home where she could get rehab for her hands. She was evaluated before she left the hospital; her Alzheimer's had progressed.

After two days in the nursing home she began to ask for a lawyer, insisting they had arrested the wrong person.

Everyone knew it was Johnny who set the fires, Johnny who stole her money, Johnny who'd crept in at night and put something in the water that changed everything and everyone but her.

# 4

# SICK LEAVE

WARM IN BED, WITH the comforter pulled up to her chin and every muscle in her body relaxed, Clarice found it impossible even to think of moving. Her eyes blinked at the clock. One minute more and then she would get up. Five more minutes and she thought she would call on the way to work and say she was running late. Then insidiously, and as warmly comforting as the feel of the sheets, she realized she was going to call in sick.

She dozed off and on until it was time to call, telling herself that she must be a little sick at least or she would have gotten out of bed already. She was not irresponsible, she did not take advantage.

After she made the call she fell back asleep for an hour and when she woke up again, she felt equally as comfortable, equally as warm, and she lay in bed for yet another hour, calmly watching the clock and adjusting the bedclothes.

When she finally got up she felt dizzy and slow and somewhat muted. She was suggestible and probably felt guilty; her body was trying to help her out by supplying a slight sense of physical disorder. The longing to get back into bed, into her nest of pillows and comforters, met her at every turn as she showered, made tea, boiled an egg.

She sat on the sofa with her tea and a magazine, propping herself up carefully as if bruised. Very soon her head began to droop and her eyes closed and her muscles grew warm and cozy and relaxed and she smiled once, affectionately, and fell asleep.

She woke up when the phone rang near her head.

It was Sally from her office. "Listen, Clarice, I'm really sorry to bother you like this, but it's that Tarbridge account, Golden Wagons? The design due this afternoon?"

Clarice rubbed her forehead with her free hand. She must have been in an awkward position, she realized; her left leg had fallen asleep. "Yes, yes," she murmured, "Golden Wagons With Golden Wheels, To Start You On Your Day."

"That's it." Sally's voice lowered. "Clarice, did you send out the wrong design, the one with a brown background? The one we did as a joke?"

Clarice frowned. "Didn't I throw that one out? Or put it in my desk? I'm sure I sent out the good one." She rubbed her leg, which still tingled.

"But we didn't pick the brown one," Sally protested. "The one we wanted was a yellow background, fields of corn, a stagecoach and horses. Not this one—the back of the box just has a cactus drawn dead center."

"Well, it's a dry cereal," Clarice said.

"That was the *joke*. What'll I do now? I just can't go into that meeting alone with this box. They'll drop us! I'll get fired!"

"Does it really look so bad?"

"Clarice, you couldn't *learn* to like it."

"Really?" Clarice said absently. "We learn to like so many things."

"That's no help," Sally said stiffly.

"Sorry. I'm a little fuzzy today. See if you can find the good design board and cut it into a rough prototype. Tell them you had a new idea over the weekend, and you're scrapping the old one. They like it when we think about them on our free time."

Sally seemed relieved. "I'm sorry, I didn't even ask. How are you feeling?"

Clarice yawned. "I'm so tired, I can't seem to stay awake. Even my leg is asleep."

"Must be some kind of bug. Your body is telling you something. Remember what I always say: Listen to your body."

"It's telling me to go to sleep again. Actually, my leg never woke up at all." She yawned into the phone. "I've never been so tired."

"Rest up! Take it easy! I won't bother you again."

"It's no bother, really," she said honestly. "Rather nice and friendly. You missed me."

"Well," Sally sounded slightly embarrassed, "it really wasn't a social call. But give me a buzz if you need anything." She hung up.

Clarice's mind drifted lazily down a path begun by Sally's call. She wasn't worried about Golden Wagons; in fact she wished that Sally would take the brown box to the meeting; she thought sardonically that if it was a really bad design, it might be a marketing asset. It would get the customer's attention, after all; and wasn't that the point? It would be new territory, almost an anti-design. The whole market took itself too seriously, that was all, it needed some sense of perspective. Gradually, she came to see the brown box (maybe a black box would be even more effective) as a deliberate statement, an act of revolt and a comment on the industry. "What does it matter anyway?" she thought serenely. "Designing stupid boxes and pretending there's no death?"

That last thought plummeted her downward. Why should she be thinking about death? She changed position, turning slightly on her right side to relieve the pressure on her left leg, which was still asleep.

But it all came down to death, finally, didn't it? Even now she could be harboring death inside her, a little sneak-thief stealing into the crisp design of her own cells and leaving a little joke box of its own. It always started with one little thing, didn't it, death? A slight shift in the pattern, at once fundamental and negligible? But then it built on it, enlarged on it, staking out more territory. And why was this leg of hers still humming with pins and needles? She must be cutting off the circulation somehow. She got up to limp around the room and clear her leg. When that didn't help, she felt a small flutter of dread invade her, just above her heart.

She took some aspirin, just in order to be doing something, and lay down in bed again, flat on her back, carefully arranging her legs and arms so that everything was relaxed and clear. She crossed her hands on her chest, then saw for a moment that this was how she would be arranged for death and moved them in horror out and along her sides. Why am I thinking about death? she wondered again.

She fell asleep, very heavily, as if dragged down into it, and when she woke the sunlight was slanted on the edge of disappearing.

She was annoyed to find out how late it was. "A whole day gone," she thought, "a whole day." She would be up all night now, and exhausted by the time she went back to work. The thought of going back to work upset her, though she liked her job as much as anybody did. It made her feel bitter, all at once. Is this what she wanted to do until she died? Was this her life?

Again she caught herself thinking about death. Normally she never really thought about it at all.

She made herself a sandwich and some tea, and turned on the television and a lot of lights. The lights helped lift her mood somewhat; she nodded when the apartment came cleanly into view.

As she watched TV she realized that she had forgotten about her leg entirely; it was now quite back to normal. She felt alert and rested. How nice it would be not to go to work again, how nice to just doze through the day—maybe not quite as much as this day—reading a book and drinking endless cups of sweetened tea.

The idea of calling in sick again surprised her. But then she thought, why not? Why not do it? Obviously, with her leg and all, she was in some strange middle territory between sickness and health, and it was wise to be cautious.

The phone rang and it was her sister calling, reminding her to come over on Saturday.

"Oh, I won't forget," Clarice told Jubilee. "I'm sure everything will be back to normal by then."

"What hasn't been normal?"

Clarice explained about calling in sick, about her leg acting strange, and how she'd slept so much, and how she kept thinking about death.

"That's what's doing it," Jubilee stated flatly. "It's wrong to think about death. Trust me on this one."

"What a strange thing to say. How could it be wrong?"

"Think about positive things. Or at the very least, neutral things. You ought to get out more, get married, have a baby."

"Then I won't die?" Clarice asked ironically.

"Then you won't die," her sister said cheerfully. "Just like me. When you have a baby you don't have much chance to think, anyhow, certainly not about your own death. How could I fit it in? I'm too busy."

"I see. No holes in your calendar?"

"No cracks in the walls. It's something to think about," she said finally, and hung up the phone.

Jubilee, of course, was a person who was always busy, had always been busy, in a chin-up, face-ahead, let's-pull-together kind of way. She tended to be at the front of lines, being both social and confident. She had always worked at jobs that required efficiency and good appearance rather than initiative; she wanted immediate rewards, the kind of easy compliments that came when she did something that no one else cared to do. In some ways Clarice looked down on her sister for her unstrained accomplishments. On the other hand, Jubilee had a husband who loved her and a small child whose birthday Clarice was invited to attend on Saturday.

Jubilee would not sleep too much, or indulge her leg in vagaries, or consider death.

Perhaps, Clarice thought at last, when it was very late and there were no longer any thumps or TV sounds from the apartments around her; perhaps it's because Jubilee has been freed from silence. It would be strange for Jubilee to sit like this in the deep pile of a silent room, and maybe silence of some sort is a precondition for death. Death has to be recognized in order to take possession, maybe Jubilee was right about that. Death was an attitude that your cells acknowledged, then acceded to. If you didn't think about it—if you were too busy—then you couldn't give any fuel to death.

By 2 a.m. Clarice had fallen asleep again, leaning back on the sofa, a soft blue light radiating towards her from the TV. She awoke with a start and a gasp; someone was pounding her leg with a hammer. She rolled off the sofa and onto the floor, grabbing her knee.

The pounding went on slowly, as if there were a pause between each stroke. She tore her clothes off to expose her leg, but there was nothing— no nerve or muscle throbbing; no bruise, not even a bump. The blue light from the TV flickered and mottled her leg, but aside from that, nothing.

She limped to the bathroom cabinet, bracing her way along the walls, and took two aspirin. She swallowed them, cried out at the next stab of pain, and took two more.

She carefully made her way back to the sofa, where she huddled next to the table with the telephone. The texture of the silence and the darkness at the windows, the knowledge that she would have to wake someone up just to hear the comfort of a voice—all this dismayed her because of the relentless, invisible pain. She would have felt better if there had been something to see—a piece of bone broken through skin, a wide gash, a sore—but there was nothing.

Through the rest of the night it hammered at her and then, suddenly, at daybreak, the pain stopped. Its absence let her recognize the small hot spot of fear now solidly inside her. Yes, something is wrong, it said, and how you approach it will determine how wrong it is.

She called her office and said she would be out again; she called her doctor and got an appointment that day.

She explained to him, slowly and carefully, what had happened. She said she had seen nothing wrong with her leg; not when it was numb nor when it was in pain. The doctor tapped little hammers at her knees and ankles and made her bend her toes and walk on the balls of her feet. She paid close attention and carried out his requests with frowning concentration.

"Well," he said after examining her, "I can't find anything obviously wrong."

"Yes," she agreed. "I can't see anything either."

"It's probably not your leg at all, you know. It's your spinal cord, or a pinched nerve or a disc. Referred pain. Pain travels along nerves, you see; the information gets transmitted, like a code, and the area that's being affected has the code for your leg, if you understand me. Anyway," he said, writing on squares of white paper, "I'm giving you a prescription for pain killers—they're strong, so take them only when needed—and the name of a specialist in back injuries. Get to him as soon as you can. Sometimes these things just disappear as mysteriously as they arrive, but you never can tell. Let me know how it turns out," he said, escorting her to the door.

She called the specialist and got an appointment for the following Monday. Having an explanation of sorts, even if it was so far unconfirmed, seemed a step forward. I don't have to consider death, she told herself, because he said this kind of referred pain is common. It's understandable and it has an underlying cause that can be discovered and fixed. She felt almost fond of her leg's foolishness, now that she considered it benign.

She called Sally later that afternoon. She was no longer falling asleep at every turn, and just resting was getting boring.

"Ah," Sally said. "I was wondering if I should call you or not. It's so hard to tell when someone calls in sick."

"If all goes well, I'll be back Monday, although I've got a doctor's appointment during the day."

"Nothing serious, I hope?"

"Seems to be a back problem. But I was wondering what happened with Golden Wagons?"

"Oh yes, that's right. Would you believe it, they rescheduled for next week? All that worry about nothing. I found the correct sketch and sent it out again."

"Oh," Clarice was disappointed. "I was curious how the brown box would have gone over. It's all in the presentation, really."

"That's fine if you're here to present it, but I don't think the idea works well for a client."

"You're right," Clarice said quickly. "It's better the way it is."

"I really think so," Sally said grumpily.

Why did I ever bother to call Sally? she thought after hanging up. We don't even like each other; why should she act warm and concerned just because I thought I was dying? She doesn't even know about that. And just as well, she concluded; that's all I'd need. She regretted the call.

On Saturday she went to her nephew's birthday party at Jubilee's house, feeling completely herself again. Jubilee had the bottom of a two-family house in Queens. The party consisted of neighbors or friends with children around Jake's age, which was five. The party quickly divided into three segments: the husbands in the backyard around the grill, the wives in the kitchen, and the children running between them.

Clarice felt conspicuous for being neither a wife or a mother. Jubilee, however, introduced her easily as a "commercial designer," and the phrase was ambiguous enough to be accurate. Clarice caught the quick look of doubt in one woman's eyes, a doubt she recognized and often felt herself. It said, Is she doing what I should have done? The talk, however, settled on children's sicknesses and playgroups and schools.

It was just when the conversation turned to gymnastics that Clarice's leg jumped. She had her legs crossed under the kitchen table, right over left, and the spasm was so strong that she hit the table hard enough to knock over two glasses and a plate of cookies.

Someone laughed and Jubilee said "Clarice?" with a warning in it, and Clarice blinked hard; her eyes were smarting. It certainly hurt, smacking into the table like that. She moved her chair away, apologized, and rubbed her knee vigorously.

"Now, why did you do that?" Jubilee asked, puzzled.

"It was an accident, Jubilee. I told you I was having trouble with my leg."

"You said pins-and-needles; you didn't say it was violent," Jubilee laughed. The women were cleaning up the spills. Clarice didn't want to move until she found out if her leg was going to continue or stop. She massaged the lump forming on her right knee.

"It's not really my leg; it's my back."

"Looked like a leg to me."

On Sunday night Clarice couldn't sleep because insects kept crawling up and down her left leg, in constant, nerve-wracking procession. She washed her leg, rubbed cream on it, poured powder on it, wrapped it in tights and socks, but still tiny legs ran up and down, maddening her.

It continued all night and she called in sick again; she could hear her voice shaking on the phone.

Her appointment was that afternoon. This doctor also tapped her with tiny hammers; he scraped along the sides of her legs, asking, "Do you feel this? And this? Do they feel the same? Push hard with your left foot, hard with your right. Does this hurt? Does this?" And she answered patiently, "I feel that. It feels the same. It doesn't hurt."

"Well, it's an interesting set of symptoms you've got," he said finally, smiling. "I suspect we're going to find inflamed nerves in your lower spine, possibly disc involvement. We'll have to do a series of tests." He paused for a moment, studying her. "Let me ask you this: with the way you've been feeling, do you think your normal activities have been compromised?"

She stared at him. "Compromised? It's hard to say what I can do anymore; it depends on my leg. Yes, I'd say compromised."

He smiled encouragement. "I just wanted to see whether we go fast or slow. The quickest way to get tests and results is to get you into a hospital. My receptionist will check into it immediately. She'll call you later, probably. And then it's full speed ahead. Don't worry. With most people it's pain, pure and simple. Your involvement has hit more diffuse territory. We'll find out why."

Clarice called her sister when she got home.

"Oh no!" Jubilee cried. "Can't you just act like nothing's happening? The hospital! Take a few days off, rest for a while."

"But that's really how it started," Clarice protested. "I just decided to call in sick, take it easy. I was fine up until then. I never knew you hated hospitals."

"Once you go in there, it's all out of your hands."

"But don't you see, it already is?"

"Clarice, think what you're doing. Do you really want this?"

Of course, Clarice thought later on, of course I don't want this. My leg is in a world of its own, experiencing things I know nothing about. I never had to think of my leg before, never! And once again, she began to suspect that it was all slipping away from her, slipping into deadly territory. Her body was straining away from her, the leg was merely a first step. If her body's trickery magnified, extended itself, so that her other leg, her arms, her heart, began to travel separate and conflicting routes in their own imagined territory, what was she to do?

The nurse called with a bed reserved for Clarice, who then called her office to give them the news. She got Sally.

"Still no better?" Sally asked.

"Worse. I'm going into the hospital tomorrow."

"That bad?" Sally asked, surprised. "What do they think it is?"

Clarice heard herself say "Nerves," and noted Sally's silence. "Nerves in my spine," she added. "Inflamed, deranged." For some reason, she thought she sounded like she was lying.

"Is that a disease?" Sally asked cautiously.

"I don't really understand what it is. They'll be doing tests. I don't know when I'll be back." She gave Sally the name of the hospital.

"Well, good luck." Sally said finally. "And I'll call you in a day or so."

"Please," Clarice said unhappily.

She surrendered to the hospital the next morning, as the nurse had told her to do. After filling out papers, she was placed in a wheelchair and taken to her room, which she shared with a woman who never spoke or moved, and who was fed through a tube in her stomach.

In the afternoon, she was taken to various rooms where she lay on tables having her spine photographed and probed. The technicians apologized for any pain they might be causing, and Clarice just waved the apologies away. She realized that the insects had left, her leg was now an ordinary leg, and it embarrassed her to hear these apologies, as if she were there under false pretenses.

On Wednesday afternoon the doctor told her that all the tests were negative, there was no sign of any irregularity. He looked at her sympathetically and sat down in the visitor's chair next to her bed. "The nervous system is very complicated. When I touch your leg, the nerves there send messages to the spinal cord, which relays the information to your brain, where the information gets translated and a response is engineered. There's nothing wrong with your leg or your spine. Logically, we have to look farther along the chain, to your brain. You see?"

Clarice twitched. "I see," she said.

"The brain is not my specialty. Another doctor will be along to look at you."

"I see," she said, attempting to seem polite and confident. When he left, she listened to the breathing of the woman in the other bed, who had never moved and who, perhaps, had no interest in the information that would make her move.

The brain doctor was small and bald and happy. He bounded into the room as if it were a stage, his fingertips lingering on the doorway as he entered.

"Strange doings?" he asked cheerfully. "Tell me about them."

Reluctantly and carefully Clarice explained what her leg had done, and the small doctor tsk'd and clucked in sympathy.

"Alarming, isn't it?" he said smiling. "But extremely interesting in a totally objective sense. Amazing, what the brain can do. The best part is that, until it all becomes too much to accept, the brain provides all sorts of explanations, too, for these goings-on. It told you everything was harmless and ordinary. Oh, how the brain loves the ordinary!" He seemed to purr to himself, then looked at her brightly. "I bet, if we had a long conversation and you were really honest with me, you'd see that strange things have been happening all along, things you took for granted, things that other people would never willingly accept. You think you see things out of the corner of your eye, but there's nothing there. You don't remember someone, but they remember you." Clarice frowned, about to protest, but he waved her objection away. "It's always a question of degree. You've translated the abnormal as slight errors in perception. But now you're on overload, you've passed the threshold. There's more information coming in than your brain can handle. There's something in that brain of yours that has taken its own path, superceded ordinary arguments. Maybe it's just a spot, a little mixed circuitry, but we can find it." He made a swift movement with his hands, almost clapping them. "I can always find it." He beamed at her and stood up. "Tests; tests first. Let's see what the diagrams in there look like." He leaned forward to tap her head once, delicately, then left.

The phone rang.

"We just had a meeting with Golden Wagons," Sally said. "They liked the design. They're very nice people, you know. I don't think they would have seen the humor in that brown box. To be honest, I never saw the humor in it either." She sounded very happy.

Is everyone happy? Clarice thought. Everyone but me? Is there some blot in my brain that keeps me from being happy?

They rolled her into machines that hit her with x-rays, sound waves, magnetic images; they took vial after vial of blood, threw lights at her eyes and checked every reflex, keeping their thoughts to themselves, making notes on charts and referring her down the line, as if they wanted to reconstruct her somewhere else.

The brain doctor came back at the end of two days, carrying her charts. "How's the leg?" he asked.

"Nothing. The past few days it's been normal."

"Ah," he said. he sat next to her and leaned forward. "We've run every test, probed you through and through. And guess what?" he smiled.

"What?"

"You have a perfectly normal brain. No clots, no tumors, no trauma of any kind. All your blood levels are normal, you react predictably and appropriately."

"Then what is it?"

"We've examined your leg, your back, your brain. Everything checks out. No elevation in any tests."

He leaned back and tapped a pen to his chin. "Of course it could be an intermittent phenomenon of some kind, too elusive to be detected yet; our tests are not perfect; excellent but not perfect. It *is* possibly organic, and maybe it's run its course. The other option, of course, is that it's not your brain creating disturbances, but your mind. It's difficult to pin down: does the mind produce the illusion of pain in your nerves, or does your nervous system *suggest* discordance to your brain? It's a dilemma. We could keep you here under observation for another week, but, quite frankly, we have no new tests to try, and no suggestion of a locality. It could be anything; it could be nothing. Where do we *look*? We've gone up the ladder, leg-spine-brain; higher than that, of course, we can only go to the mind; and where do we locate the trouble there: perception, ideation, evaluation? Or do we declare that the mind is sound and the trouble is external: God, the devil, or manipulative space aliens? You see the problem: you insist your body is not working properly. We insist it is." He raised his eyebrows and smiled at the same time, suggesting to Clarice both sympathy and forgiveness.

"Then what do I do?" Clarice asked.

"My only advice is to stop having these symptoms." He continued to smile as Clarice stared at him. "You understand?"

"You're saying that this is a personal problem." She spoke slowly.

"Perhaps your imagination needs an increased outlet, or your concept of boundaries needs to be redrawn. Or maybe it's your sense of time that's off; maybe you don't recognize the end of a sensation. Whatever it is, I'm confident that the solution lies outside medicine." He gazed at her while he spoke, with an almost palpable sympathy.

"Then it doesn't exist, this pain," she said weakly

"Or, let's say, not yet. At any rate, you can go home now."

Clarice left the hospital with a confused determination to think of her leg as an object only, as an impetuous, controllable force. It was not death, she told herself, it had nothing to do with death, and perhaps those very thoughts of death were also just unallied symptoms, pointing nowhere.

She got out of the hospital on Friday and on Saturday went to see Jubilee. She meant to turn right on the block that led to the train station, but turned unaccountably left. It was a few minutes before she noticed her error, and she had to concentrate in order to turn around and get to her train. On the ride she thought how tedious it was. And how nice it would have been for Jubilee to come see her, instead of the other way around.

"You look fit as a fiddle," Jubilee said when she saw her. "Wasn't I right?"

"About what?"

"Doctors don't do any good, hospitals won't do any good. Don't let them get you."

"They didn't do anything, Jubilee. They said they couldn't do anything for me." She hoped for sympathy or advice, something related to her, anyway, some clue to her own life that she was, perhaps, too close to see.

"But I bet you'll get the bills anyway," Jubilee said sharply. "You always have to pay."

"I have insurance," Clarice said mildly.

"Oh well, I don't want an argument, I'm just glad you're all right." She grinned a big grin at Clarice, who grinned back, thinking, Well, it really didn't make much difference to Jubilee one way or the other.

Jubilee talked about what her husband had said, what her child had said, what a friend had said, and Clarice nodded, thinking: Of course, none of this is important to me. She longed to move into the territory that was important to her, but, even thinking about it hard, she couldn't. The strangeness of her leg and the soft rustle of death: these were important, but they were promptings or hints, not causes.

She listened to Jubilee vaguely and asked, as if casually, "But what does all this mean to you?"

Jubilee blinked, paused, said, "It means what it is. Things are what they seem: a family, a child, a life." She smiled. "A shopping list, a recipe, a question. They're all what they seem to be."

"Ah," Clarice said, and she believed for a moment that Jubilee was entirely right, the world was calmly transparent, and nobody died. Suddenly she got up and said, "I have to go."

"Go?" Jubilee was surprised. "Go where? You just got here."

"I have to go somewhere," Clarice answered, heading firmly for the door. "My leg is restless. I have something to do." She stopped, turned around, and kissed Jubilee on the cheek. "Don't worry, it's nothing personal."

"Have I said something? I didn't mean to say something." Jubilee was alarmed. "You always stay to dinner."

"I have to go."

She left quickly and thought, rather happily, I blamed it on my leg.

She got to the station, took the train to the city, and began to walk around, without purpose or direction. She walked to the river on the west side, looking intently, and then to the east side, walking down to the bottom of Manhattan, out to where the river widened to Buttermilk Channel, looking off to Ellis Island, Staten Island, Brooklyn opening out in front of her, and beyond them, whipping up a furious wind, the ocean.

She walked back and forth along the promenade, marching with her head turned out to sea. Her leg, she thought at first, was driving her forward, but the feeling of being driven crept through her until it changed into a languorous feeling of good will and she stopped, finally, and just leaned against the guardrail staring out to sea. Ships passed, both small and large, and seagulls screamed triumphantly of far possibilities. They screamed with wild unconscious certainty, although she didn't know how often and how far they went to sea. Did they always stay on the edge of the unknown, as she did now, on the border of an illness without credentials? She thought again of death and how, if it really had laid its first marks on her, the only truly surprising thing in her life would be her discredited dying, stubbornly failing as everyone declared she was perfectly fine.

Her disease—though no one else saw it, she knew it was there—would continue, peremptory and humiliating. Perhaps it would take her over, bit by bit, insistently kicking as she tried to stay polite. She would be deprived of defiance, irony, or awe, things she had never required before and which now struck her as necessary and ordained.

How she loved the wind whipping up and the suggestion of rain and the remote cry of the birds and the outside view of the boats leaving, a boat blowing its horn.

She could return to work as if nothing was happening, deny this horrifying and interesting disease. That would be not so much harmful and wasteful as narrow, a life lived with her jaw clenched, a death gained under ordinary circumstances. Or she could go where all the deaths were exotic deaths, where obscure and even obscene diseases were real, and respectfully addressed as real.

She walked home, sliding between the figures hurrying around her, sliding like a knife, cutting it all away.

She went home and packed her bags, putting in too much, of course, but she didn't know where she was going and the excess could always be discarded. She went through her papers, finalizing bills. She called Jubilee, who understood none of it, and asked her to sell the furniture and all her small, careful goods, in any way she could.

She finalized all her money on Monday, leaving Jubilee in charge of everything that was left. She made her calls, resigning her job, telling a surprised Sally goodbye and buying spare toothbrushes with joy. She bought a ticket for South America, and travel guides for other continents, and felt remarkably light. With each step she felt lighter, relieved of inessential details, as if she were casting off lines she had never noticed detaining her. She got shots for diseases with names, her arms swollen and her head swimming, and by Thursday she had bid goodbye to Jubilee and stood, her heart pounding, on a ramp that led to an airplane waiting almost incidentally for her. All of it seemed unusual, amusing, and profoundly good. Tomorrow she would look out on a world with a different shaft of sunlight falling on it, a different cadence of speech, with brand-new colors flashing from the treetops, and she would stride into it, leg kicking or dragging or unnoticed, overlooked in the onrush of new sensations, her feet striking new land, radiant land, and dust—foreign, senseless, alien dust—covering her straight up to her knees and tinging the taste of her smile in a new world.

$$5$$

# FRANKIE THE MOB

M Y MOTHER'S YOUNGER HALF-BROTHER, Frank, was notorious. He had a job for a long time "in cement," where he robbed his customers, beat up a few, lost a lot of money for people who only had a little money. In other words, scum. We always called him "Frankie" rather than Uncle Frankie, probably because he told us to. He wasn't impressed with family unless it suited him. He was exciting when we were kids; he did the unexpected. Taking us for a ride and not telling anyone; giving us twenty-dollar bills that made everyone check their wallets; bringing expensive electronics for presents, like TVs, cameras, computers. Our parents got a strained look on their faces about that, but we had to keep it because if it was "hot" they couldn't return it anywhere and no one wanted to piss Frankie off. He had scars and sometimes came in with stained shirts whose color caught my mother's eye. "Is that blood?" she'd ask, and Frankie would say, "Maybe someone's," and laugh.

He was in prison ("away" we were told) a few times when we were young, and when we grew up we learned enough to be both on our guard around him and utterly fascinated. "Our uncle the mobster," we told our friends. "Our uncle the con." We were proud of him.

Until he started coming around unannounced, asking to use the house for a meeting, and would we mind leaving? That got creepy. We would return when he said, sneaking around on tiptoe, afraid we'd find something—a ring, a toe, something—that would confirm our fears.

He did kill someone but they couldn't make it intentional, so he went away but not forever. By then, my sister and I had grown up and he wasn't a good anecdote anymore. Our parents changed the locks twice a year, even after he was in prison, because we never knew *who* he'd brought to the house, who might have gotten in and would come in again. My parents finally sold the house and moved somewhere else, but the habit of changing locks is hard to break. It wasn't until after my father died, and my mother moved into a senior citizens' facility, that the whole lock business changed. There was a guard at the door and an intercom system. And besides, she had actually moved twice after my father died; it was hard to think Frankie would find her.

Of course I thought she wouldn't want him to. But that was when she still had her senses.

And then one day, my mother said, "Frankie was here. He brought me mums. I've never liked mums. And it isn't even the season for them. But you know Frankie. Probably took them off some funeral arrangement." She winked at me and smiled comfortably.

"I thought you didn't like Frankie," I said after a pause.

"Me?" she asked, astonished. "Why he's a card, he really is. Always something hopping when Frankie's around. Why wouldn't I like him?" She looked at me as if I were an idiot.

"He stole your jewelry, didn't he? A long time ago?"

"Oh, that?" She waved the thought away. "That was junk anyway and besides," she brightened up, "I think Frankie gave it to me to begin with."

She became convinced. "Why yes. So maybe he just lent it to me after all." A fond smile. "That Frankie!"

❊ ❊ ❊

Now, APPARENTLY, FRANKIE WAS okay; or maybe she just had the memory of Frankie before she began to fear him. I didn't know if she was seeing the real Frankie and couldn't remember what he'd done, or an imaginary Frankie, a young Frankie who might still get his act together.

Odd, isn't it, that people might look at you and see a different version of you?

Uncle Frankie did have a son, Sonny. I hadn't seen him in years; his mother disappeared with him one night; we had all sorts of speculation about it. Were they dead? In witness protection? Had they run off with a different mobster? We politely asked Uncle Frankie how things were; we said we needed their address for Christmas and birthday cards. Uncle Frankie said, Yeah, later, he didn't have it on him at the time; everyone knew he couldn't remember numbers.

❊ ❊ ❊

I WAS TELLING MY husband, Michael, all of this one night when I noticed him frowning and tapping his knee.

Maybe Michael was tired of hearing me talk. "Is there dinner?" he asked. "I'm hungry."

"Of course there's dinner," I said, thinking quickly. Ten minutes or so to cook pasta, some frozen sauce and stuff to microwave. I'd get a salad going and it will look like I had a plan. "Did you bring wine?" I joked.

"Well, your Uncle Frankie," he began.

"That story!"

"I don't know if your mother saw him, but I did," he said. "He's in bad shape, liver's all shot, gone yellow and spotted with it." He raised his voice as I went to the kitchen. "He's dying," Michael said, almost a shout.

"Good for him," I said to myself. "Mother will be shocked," I yelled back to Michael.

"So don't tell her; she doesn't know anything half the time."

Easy enough to say but when you're faced with your mother, half of her mind gone, you keep grasping for something to say, some little scrap that will prop up a memory, you bring up absurd things, stupid things, things so old you can barely stay awake to mention them. So Frankie was bound to come up.

I shook a bottle of dressing, poured it over two bowls of romaine lettuce chopped up just the way Michael likes it. "Soup's on," I yelled, setting out the flatware and the glasses. "Ice water? Milk and roses? What's your pleasure?"

"I'll have a beer. We have a beer, right?"

"We have a beer," I admitted. "So how did you run into Frankie? You two were never friends."

"He killed my dog," he said, munching on a leaf. I love that about him, how he likes his greenery.

And old story. "That would put me off," I agreed.

He raised his eyebrows at me. Sometimes he doesn't like my humor. "You hate someone, you keep an eye out. All these years, I've been tracking him."

"Good heavens," I said. "Sounds like you want to get even."

"Yes," he said, shoveling greens in his mouth. "I intend to get even. Not much fun when he can fight back. But now, when he's sick—why it will mean more to him, won't it? When he feels helpless? Like a kid with a dead dog? You see what I'm saying?"

"I do," I said. "I see what you're saying."

Well, I called my sister, Lily, and told her all about it. Lily lives way out in the desert, as far away from anyone as she can. She has an adobe house and she paints big bold pictures. I told her that's already been done, but she said she's not pretentious and happy to be an imitator. There are lots of imitation buyers, she said. Paying real money.

I guess she was lucky not to be bothered with talent.

"Frankie?" she asked.

"Yes, Frankie. I just said that." My sister has a habit of tuning me out, selectively.

"I assumed he was dead. Or at least, I never think about him. He's sick? So what? He deserves what he gets."

"Well, it's really Michael I'm worried about. He wants to get even."

"It's because of the dog, right?"

Everyone knew about that. All the kids hung out together and we roamed all over the neighborhood. Michael lived around the corner and he was always coming around with his dog, Spider, named after Michael's favorite comic book, Spider-Man. We lived in a quiet, working-class neighborhood in Brooklyn. Most of the houses had small yards in front, and Spider had a habit of running over to Frankie's yard and barking. Like it was personal.

Spider was often off the leash, and Uncle Frankie eventually put out some meat with sleeping pills in it. He claimed that he only meant to teach the dog a lesson. Or he claimed that if the meat was bad, how come he'd had a hamburger and didn't get sick? And he convinced some of us; after all, who would kill a nice friendly dog like Spider? Michael's father called the police, and the neighborhood saw Frankie on the street, leaning into the police car, straightening up and shrugging his shoulders, his big head wagging slowly from side to side. No, no, not me, not my style. That's what I imagined.

And it maybe wasn't his style, but Michael believed it was murder. For a while, he would bring hamburgers over in a bag, leaking juices, and hang

them on Uncle Frankie's door. I saw Frankie pause once, study the current
burger, and eat it. He licked his fingers when he was done.

❀ ❀ ❀

MY MOTHER SOMETIMES CALLED my husband Frankie, and he always
corrected her. She would appear puzzled and look at him steadily. Then
she'd smile; it was one of his jokes, of course. She'd nod and ask what his
name was today, and my husband would growl and say, "Some as yester-
day. Michael." But that was close to the end, before she gave up talking
altogether, when no one's names mattered anymore.

But I remember once she scolded me, when I was a girl, about the way
the children always got excited when Frankie came over to visit. She'd
hear us all telling stories about the crimes he'd committed, the weapons
he had. The criminals he hung out with, that everyone knew about—
Vinny Pizza, Shady Al, Ponte One-Eye. We loved the names. We gave
each other gangster names. Mickey Two-Punch. Lily Quick-Hands. I was
Patty Two-Face, because I could tell the best lies. When it was just us kids
together, we'd call him Frankie the Mob.

"You kids shouldn't idolize him," my mother snapped. "He's not a
good man. And it's not romantic, and if you grow up to be like him you'll
spend your time in prison or dead. He takes advantage of poor people and
he makes everyone look over their shoulder, because we don't know what
he'll do next."

"It's like the movies," I said in defense. "He's not dull and boring. I
don't want to grow up dull and boring."

"You'll be lucky if you do," she sniffed. "His wife and son are gone,
he's in and out of prison, you don't know the half of what he's done and
besides—he doesn't even know your name! That's how much you matter
to him. Listen, I don't give you a lot of advice, but remember this. His life
is exciting, but it isn't good. It can't be good. He's always scheming and

he looks at people to see what he can get from them. That's the devil for you. He's not glamorous. Jail isn't glamorous. He's a man who takes things away from people not because he needs it even, but just because he likes them to know he can do it. If you have something that interests him, he'll take it. Because he wants you to think you'll never be safe unless you kneel down to him. And even then, you'll never be safe."

Which was true, of course, because here he was, dying, and we still weren't safe.

My husband came home late a few times, claiming he'd gone out for a drink with the guys. He did that. "And Frankie?" I asked once or twice. "What did you decide about him?"

"I'm still thinking," he said.

But there was the slightest smirk around his mouth.

❖ ❖ ❖

"FRANKIE WAS HERE AGAIN," my mother said.

"How come he's visiting all of a sudden? He only does it when he wants something."

"Forgive and forget," my mother said vaguely. She was well on her way to forgetting; it was easy for her.

"So what did he say?"

"Aliens," my mother said firmly. "Those aliens are bothering him."

I had to think about that. My mother had been having hallucinations lately, but nothing about aliens. "Foreigners?" I guessed.

My mother looked at me steadily, thinking it through. "What? What does that mean? Are the Russians moving in? I know they moved in over at Ginny's neighborhood. I haven't seen them."

"What did Frankie say?" I was trying to be patient. I was trying to sort out her latest ideas.

"Someone keeps stealing his car."

I had to stay with that a bit before I answered. "Really? And what do you mean that they keep stealing it? Do they bring it back or something?"

"He called the police the first time—can you imagine? Frankie? I told him someday he'd land in jail, he takes so many chances."

"He *was* in jail. For six years."

She frowned. "That can't be true. He's wild but they don't put you in jail for being wild. He's young. He'll grow out of it."

He was in his late sixties. Of course that would seem young to her. But I didn't think she remembered, or saw, his current age.

"And what did the police say?"

"They found it around the corner. No damage, he said. The cops looked at him like he was forgetful. Well, you know," she said, suddenly leaning towards me and whispering. "It runs in his family, craziness does. His mother had it."

"Your mother?"

She took her time again, digesting it, but it was apparently hard to hold on to. "And it happened again. That's why he came to see me," she said triumphantly. "To ask if I borrowed his car." She gave a short laugh. "Loony. I have a perfectly good car of my own." She shook her head sympathetically. "I think he's getting a little confused."

It was great to imagine Frankie's stony stare as the cops brought the car back and told him it was around the corner. Cops can have stony stares too; so I pictured each one looking at the other like he was looking at an idiot.

❈ ❈ ❈

"So you're moving his car around?" I asked Michael later that day. He'd gotten home on time. Maybe he knew Uncle Frankie's schedule well enough by now that he could vary when he moved the car.

Michael put a forkful of food into his mouth and chewed thoroughly. He raised his hand to make me wait. Then he put his fork down and looked at me thoughtfully. "Is he losing it?" he asked.

"Please assume you're not talking to a fool," I said. I crossed my arms and glared. I was good at body language.

He smiled at me. "After all he's done, it's not very much, is it?"

"He's an old man."

"He only got caught once. And you know he did a lot more than that. You know people suffered."

"This isn't about those people. This is about your dog."

"It's about all of it. It's about how we all loved him because he was a gangster. No one ever admitted he was just a damn selfish shill."

It was true, of course. We did love him for his aura, for his glamour, for the stories. "I know," I said finally. "I know. But he's an old man now."

"He took advantage of old people in particular," my husband said, picking up another bit of food. "He took their money. He didn't care and he didn't get caught, most of the time. This is just an annoyance to him."

"Mom thinks he's getting forgetful."

Michael held my eyes for a moment. "That wouldn't be fair," he said. "I really want him to remember everything he did. I want him to wonder who's doing this, and why. I want him to flip through the cards in his head, trying to sort it all out. He won't think of me. I was a kid. He could hurt kids, but kids were forgettable." He wiped his mouth. "This is small potatoes."

I thought about it for a day or two. I felt bad because Frankie was old and apparently ill. But it was true—so were some of the people he ripped off. He had spent his years taking advantage, misleading, ripping off. He had no right to a safe old age.

I went to see Frankie a few days later. I knocked on his door and an old man shuffled out. He was grizzled, and his eyes sagged. He looked at me warily as he answered the door.

"Hi," I said. "I live around the corner. I thought it was only right to tell you before I told the police. You hit my dog," I said.

"No, I didn't," he said heavily. "I didn't hit anything."

"I saw your car hit my dog. I took him to the vet. They had to put him down."

"Not me," he said. "Someone's been taking my car."

"I'm filing a report," I said. "I'm going to the police. I just thought I'd tell you. I have a camera outside my house. I have the tape showing your car hitting my dog, and leaving."

"Not me," he said. "I don't know where my car is half the time. Someone keeps taking it. I put up a camera, too," he said, gesturing to a camera on the corner of his house. "It keeps getting painted over."

"I just wanted to tell you first," I said, continuing my theme. "Someone else saw your car side-swipe their car. And there are tire tracks on Simona's lawn. If you can't handle a car anymore, you should stop driving it."

"I can handle a car," he protested.

"Sometimes it's hard to admit," I said. "Like with my mother. We had to hide her keys for a while. Then she ran into a stop sign and the cops suspended her license. Maybe it runs in the family."

He took a closer look at me. "Patty?"

"Of course Patty. You didn't recognize me?" I asked. He hadn't seen me in years by that point, and I had changed my hair color.

It must have unnerved him because he shut the door quickly after muttering he wasn't the crazy one, not yet he wasn't. I felt guilty; I had to fight that feeling of guilt. Of course what I was doing was wrong; it wasn't right to use a disease as a toy.

But there was a reason for it, I told myself. My mother was making Frankie into a nice guy: all right, anything that gave her the illusion of peace was fine. But he hadn't seen her in years; I had no doubt that he had a scheme of some sort he was playing out on her. "I'm a little short on cash," I could imagine him saying, laughing, to my mother. Hoping to be remembered in her will. It hadn't occurred to him that she was no longer competent to change her will. Whatever it was, he would only show up when he had a plan of some kind that would keep him going for a little longer.

And Michael was right. Over the years, Frankie had preyed on weaker people, using them without a look back. He'd congratulated himself on "pulling a fast one." As if that was the secret to life.

But, too, my husband was involved, and he wasn't necessarily good at covering himself. Even though Frankie was a monster and he was failing and buddies ran fast from dying monsters, he still might have a few favors to call in, a few toughs who would figure out what was going on and make sure Michael was stopped. So it was up to me to move it faster, to get to the end before Frankie's thugs caught Michael and made him pay.

✻ ✻ ✻

WITHIN A WEEK, FRANKIE was in an accident. I heard it from his neighbor, Milo, across the street. Milo was old-fashioned; he sat outside on his porch and watched everything around him.

Frankie's car had gone missing again and rather than call the police, Frankie had walked around the blocks until he found it. Milo saw Frankie turn the corner and then there was a loud pop and Frankie plowed into a streetlight, knocking it over.

"His tire burst," Milo said. "A really loud pop. I called 911, got the police and an ambulance."

I told Michael, who looked completely satisfied with the story. "Nice," he said.

"So you screwed with his tire?"

"I never touched his tire," he said.

He was right about that. Turns out that whoever had moved his car had also placed a single firecracker on the top of the carburetor; when the engine got hot, the firecracker went off. I have to admire the calculations involved in figuring out how far away the car had to be in order for the firecracker to go off before he got home again.

"It was a firecracker," I told my husband, who tried to look surprised.

"Must have sounded like a gun," he grunted. "Funny. You wouldn't think a gunshot would startle Frankie."

And it went like that. The car stayed where it was for weeks, until Frankie got relaxed. And then someone put sugar in his gas tank.

❈ ❈ ❈

THE CAR SAT IN his driveway, untouched. Milo called the police when he hadn't seen Frankie for a few days; they kicked in the door when he didn't answer and found him fast asleep in his bed. He was on new medication that made him tired.

Police! Breaking into his place! It was lovely.

❈ ❈ ❈

MY MOTHER BEGAN TO drift away. I asked her if Frankie had been by, and she looked at me steadily, not quite studying me. She was losing her ability to connect. "Mom," I said. "Would you like to go outside? It's a lovely day."

That same steady look again. Was she trying to decode each word? Her eyelids came down. Her breathing got quieter. I sat by her bedside, remembering when she was sturdy and young and strong and had nothing but contempt for Frankie, who once I think tried to appease her by bringing me a puppy. It was black and fluffy and had little brown eyes and sharp little teeth. It wasn't housebroken, and it peed everywhere. My mother insisted we find it a new home.

That's right. It went to Michael. The dog Frankie killed was the gift Frankie had given us. Maybe it wasn't about the barking after all. Maybe Frankie had a secret hidden spot where he thought about what he could do to get his half-sister's family to take him in, to like him. And he had watched as the gift was thrown away.

Maybe that was the real Frankie, that gift-giver. Maybe he had suffered whenever he tried to appease someone, suffered by never knowing what was the gesture that would stick.

Maybe.

I looked at the guest book after I left my mother that day. It went back a full month. Frankie had been there only once. She had imagined the other visits. She had hoped for them. In her last days, she had gone back to him, perhaps even forgetting who I was. Frankie was the one who was on her mind.

I would visit Frankie soon. I would see how he was doing, suggest he visit my mother before it was too late, and on the way out, after he'd seen me to the door and then closed it and turned back into the darkness of his hallway—I'd go and unscrew the nuts on one tire.

With any luck, he'd hit something hard.

# 6

# ROAD WORK

OH I HAVE TO be very careful. There are spare keys everywhere now: under the pot by the doorway, taped to the railing around the garage, attached with a magnetic case to the inside of the front tire of my car. I've locked myself out three times; that's why there are so many spares. Which one will I remember the next time? I'm like a squirrel burying nuts. Squirrels don't remember every last acorn, do they? I've even considered taping one to the maze of signs posted by the Blue Dot Construction Company since I seem to pass their signs wherever I go.

I'm crafty now instead of smart. I can't remember names, even though I do exactly what the memory books say: repeat their names three times in the introductory conversations. "Hello, Melissa," I say. "I happen to like the name Melissa. In fact, as a child, I had a goldfish named Melissa." There. Three times. It's supposed to stick.

Unfortunately, I'm with a fellow employee at the time. This fellow employee grunts and says, "I thought you had a goldfish named Mike."

I blink at him. That's easy. His name is Mike. "I had them both," I say charmingly. "A mated pair. My two favorite names."

Melissa looked at me with an air of faint perplexity. "I like goldfish," I said. "For a while I named them all the same thing, but then I could never tell one from the other."

"That's enough for me," Mike said, rolling his eyes. "I can't stand goldfish stories."

Melissa's eyes tracked Mike as he left, then returned to me.

"You're new here," I said. "Melissa. But we've all been new hires at least once, so don't worry, you'll get over it."

"My name's Jennifer," she said stiffly. "And you know that perfectly well."

"My mistake." I smiled ruefully. "Slight cold in my ear, I should see someone about it." I looked at her, one of those glancing, piercing, friendly looks. She had a comfortable face, though right now it looked a little annoyed. She would be quite attractive, if a little worn, when she stopped frowning.

"I didn't know you'd be here," she said, sotto voce.

That surprised me; it was my turn to frown. "Where else would I be?" For a moment I thought she knew about my limp brain; for a moment I thought I was exposed.

"I'm sure you haven't forgotten me," she said stiffly, and I relaxed. Injured pride, that's all it was!

"Forget you, Melissa?" I wheedled. "Could anyone?"

"My name is Jennifer," she snarled, and turned on the ball of her left foot, and was gone. It was a lovely move.

I smiled at her back in a friendly, engaging way. I laughed out loud. The person who isn't upset is always the winner, and I wasn't the least upset. My score.

I'm the manager of a department that processes and distributes the paychecks. Well of course it's called Payroll and that's pretty self-explanatory. Most of the work is computerized now, and I've been here so long that I'm computerized too. The fact that the basics haven't changed—weeks in the year, math formulas, tax regulations—means that I can be brave and come to work each day, and no one really notices that half of my mind is gone.

Of course I don't know if it's half, or more, or less. I could only judge that if I had my former mind and my current mind next to each other. I could call one "apples" and the other one "oranges."

The other reason no one is sure anything is wrong is because I smile cheerfully, I laugh at jokes, I shake hands, I clasp their elbows, I wink. These are things that are indifferent to IQ. It doesn't matter if I can't do higher math, as long as the programs can. And I treat everyone equally well because, quite frankly, I forget who I'm mad at.

I'm 45 years old. I've had a brain event and I took a little extended leave for a while. I have a notebook with the questions I always ask my doctors, and the gist of their answers. My questions are basically: What happened? and: What will happen? I cheer up when I read questions like this in my notebook, they seem very efficient, very capable. I have a harder time with the answers, which consist mostly of highlight phrases such as "cognitive dissociation, ischemic dissonance, presumed (in)capacity." I know I understood them at the time or I wouldn't have written anything down; or maybe I meant to look them up later. In fact, I think I did look them up later. There were some very hard, unfriendly sentences involved.

The doctor told me it wasn't as bad as I imagined. "See?" he said. "You can hold a perfectly normal conversation." I wrote that down.

My little department has been working perfectly well for the 20 years I've been here. We didn't have computers like we do now, when I started; we had punch cards, which I still prefer to computers. You can look at a punch card; I like that. You can hold it. These programs, though—I like to say they don't exist in the physical world and my bet is, not in the spiritual world either.

Sometime later, Jennifer came back with her forms filled out and stood by my desk, slapping them gently against her left hand. It's probably a nervous gesture; most people are nervous around Payroll.

"Hi, Melissa," I said, then quickly added, "Jennifer." That kind of slip—it's more like a blurt—happens to me often now. It's a kind of free association, a sort of say-what-comes-to-mind thing. My mind's like a conveyor belt of fragments. When I open my mouth sometimes a box slips off. Or maybe I did know a Melissa once, and she looked like Jennifer. Perhaps, even, I had a goldfish who looked like Jennifer but I called it Melissa. I thought I made the whole goldfish thing up, but maybe I didn't.

My husband, Carlos, says it's really not that noticeable. "I don't notice anything, really," he said, patting my arm. "Except for that fire. That fire was a little scary."

That was just a little kitchen grease fire. He yelled a little and put it out. The phone had rung while I was frying and he hadn't answered it, so I did.

I've found, indeed, that my problem is an almost organic need for linear living. I mean, if I get interrupted I go with the interruption; whatever I was doing ceases to exist.

"Well, that's true for everyone, to a certain extent," Carlos said. This was after the fire, when he'd settled down again. Really, the worst of it was that the kitchen would need to be painted, but it frightened us both, of course. I was in despair. It was the thing, finally, that drove me to the doctors, who also said, "That's normal enough."

It would be much easier if I had a broken arm rather than a broken brain. They're not good at broken brains here in this small town. And I've got to be grateful that it's a small town with pretty much the same deal every day.

At least the eye doctor had a little sympathy when I told him I saw things darting at me, that's why I ducked during the welcome home party our neighbors gave, and knocked the drinks over.

"Floaters," he said, in a comforting, agreeable tone. "Happens to a lot of people our age. There's nothing really out there, it's at the back of your eye that everything's happening."

A real physical explanation of something no one else can see; I liked that. Verification of something only I can verify. A blessing.

"Maybe that's why you always seem to flinch when I scratch my head," Carlos said.

"Sometimes it looks like you're going to hit me," I answered.

❋ ❋ ❋

I ENCOUNTERED A SMALL problem the next week about the deductions. There was a new tax table; they'd changed the rates. I'd entered everything in plenty of time, and I'm almost perfectly sure I tested the results; it's the kind of thing I would do, and I'm pretty sure I still do the things I would do. I mean, what else would I do—the things Carlos does? The things a stranger would do? Some things just don't make sense when you examine them too closely.

Obviously the program was flawed, or there was one of those computer viruses that break out on a particular date (which would explain why the program worked perfectly fine when I probably checked it, and then didn't work at all). Not everyone noticed right away, but that new employee did. New employees always examine their paychecks so carefully.

And (it's just the way these things go), with everyone else the error was pennies; with her it was hundreds of dollars.

She said (her face pinched, her voice wobbly), "There's been some mistake." She opened the pay envelope carefully and spread out the details. She had markings in red pen and blue pen all over it.

"Oh yes," I said. "Some trouble with the program." I laughed. "Not everyone noticed, though. Not everyone looked as closely as you."

A little bit of red spread over her neck. Her face got even stiffer. "My entire paycheck is less than $200." She waited.

I waited too.

"It's insulting," she said finally.

"Well, it's an *error*," I pointed out. "And I'm correcting the errors. God knows what that programmer was thinking." I pitched my voice in a friendly light tone. I was charming.

She stared at me. I looked her over, since it was her turn to respond. All I knew from her file was that she was a few years (not much) younger than I; that we had worked for the same company once, almost 20 years earlier. Not in the same department, though. It wasn't that unusual; there were a few major employers in the area and a lot of us found ourselves with similar resumes. I didn't remember her.

"Do you want me to leave?" she asked stiffly.

"Oh no, just give me a minute. I'll have a new check for you right away, I already adjusted the program. I'll just hit Print. That always does it."

"I don't mean 'here' here," she said, frowning in frustration. "I meant the job. Do you want me to quit?"

"Why would I want you to quit?" I examined her even more closely. She looked to me like she should be surrounded by a doorway. What an odd thought. Maybe framed is what I meant, but why would I mean it? She did look a little familiar, if I strained through twenty years of changes (her) and a damaged brain (me).

"Some people carry grudges," she answered meaningfully. Her eyes were bright and pointed.

She seemed to expect a reaction from me. "Should I have a grudge against you?" I asked.

She dropped her eyes and frowned. We listened, together, to the sound of the printer. I got the check when it was done and signed it.

She accepted it without a word and turned to the door. "Did something happen when we worked together before?" I asked. "Did something go wrong?"

Her body was halfway out the door when she turned her head around and gaped at me. Her mouth hung open and her eyebrows shot up. Then she turned and left, without a word.

Some time after that, I noticed that a few checks were missing. The system we use feeds sheets of bank-issued checks into the printer, where they wait until I key in such information as date, payee, amount, account number. The sheets hold numbered checks; if one was misprinted or ruined, it was voided. Each number was accounted for, which was why the program itself didn't just print out a check and number it.

And suddenly I noticed that nine checks were missing. On the day I discovered it, I just laid low. I organized my desk and then the print trolley. Then I hit the computer. The fact that it was missing nine checks meant it could be a transposition (I was good at math; an error in units of nine was almost always a transposition).

I mentioned it to Carlos that night, and he was disturbed, which made me cheerful in defense, I suppose. At any rate we had an argument. I'm not exactly sure what it was about now; in fact, I don't think I understood it at the time. One thing that struck me was, he said: "It's just the kind thing you always do."

Do I? I was insulted; I couldn't remember ever doing anything like this before. And which part of "this" did he mean: losing checks, covering up, being confident it would all work out; worrying him needlessly?

Not only did that bother me, but I began to think I was in trouble. I wasn't sure what kind of trouble, but I had to give up on the transposition, which was a theoretical thing and didn't account for the physical reality. Had I lost the checks? Had someone stolen them? Had I written them out and deleted the entries? Things looked bleak, though I would forget all about it for a while, only to be drawn up short with remembering.

This wasn't helped when I saw the VP of Finance standing at my desk soon after.

"Oh," I said, "Bill."

He sighed. "It's still Phil. It's always been Phil."

I was about to make a joke about failing memory, but then I stopped myself. It might not be appropriate, considering he was my boss. "You remind me," I began.

"Yes, yes, I know," he interrupted. "Your goldfish Bill. Let me get to the point quickly because I need your help on something."

I relaxed.

"I got a complaint about you." My back snapped into place. "I've never had a complaint about you before, and from what I heard, it's a personal situation."

"Personal?"

"You and Jennifer. I understand you have a past, that there was a... situation."

"A situation?"

He hemmed and hawed and shuffled and stroked his head. "She told me some of it. I don't really want to know your side. I mean, the sides don't matter." He took a deep breath. "It's just, now that she's here, you've got to live with it. I'll move her somewhere else, but not just yet, it would be too obvious. So. Can you handle it, can you calm down?"

"I'm calm. I'm always calm. You know that. What did she say?"

"Said you messed with her paycheck. That kind of thing's actionable."

"We had a program glitch. It's the patched version and there was something wrong with it. I had to re-do her check. I guess hers was worse because it was her first check, you know; there was no database on her."

"It's a bad situation," he said, "when you've got history together."

"Situation" again. Small wonder that he was always a VP, never a P. He was irritating me, so I gave him a brilliant big-eyed smile. "It's not much," I assured him. "We worked together."

"All three of you worked together," he said gruffly. "They warn you about that kind of thing. Triangles, affairs with co-workers." He shook his head regretfully. "I know it was a long time ago, but I guess no one really gets over 'the other woman,' do they?" He blinked and looked uncomfortable. "Sorry. Not my business. Just keep your hands clean and sit it out." He nodded and was gone.

Leaving me stunned. There was something about a triangle, an affair, straining like a beast in a box to get out. No, not a beast. A small weak thing, barely scratching, hardly pleading.

What a poor thing memory is, constantly being overlaid and pushed down under all the weight of new experiences. I understand it's not https://123sonography.com/sites/default/files/styles/article_image/ public/image/images/xshutterstock_575199331,P20sick,P20astronaut. jpg,qitok=Jl3_xAhh.pagespeed.ic.t0zZujgqI_.webp considered magical anymore, memories are physically branded in the brain so that a tiny wire and brief current applied spot by spot in the brain will recall exactly what was stored there: the scent of apples on a particular tree, wet wool in school, the first real kiss.

But I have no electric prod, and the stuff is gone haywire, misplaced, out of index. Which one was I in this triangle? Injured or injuring, abandoned or cherished? Who was the man?

I tried very hard to recall Jennifer. I tried to trigger her by association. I examined the contents of my purse first, pulling out things to see what I remembered. I knew my name, my address, and my birth date, where I worked, what I looked like. I had checks, credit cards, a health plan ID, driver's license, address book and calendar. I went through the address book. Jennifer wasn't in it. And there were a lot of names I didn't recognize; I didn't dwell on that. I found a store credit and a clipping of a review for an unfamiliar movie. Had I seen it?

Jennifer knocked on the door—or rather, since there wasn't a door, only a doorway, she knocked on the doorway. I wondered if I'd found her in flagrante delicto with someone I loved, or whether I'd been told, and if so, by whom? She wanted a form for direct deposit to her checking account. We would all have been much younger then, when it happened. I'm sure I recovered quite well, over time. It's true what they say about time.

That night I cuddled next to Carlos on the sofa. "We're lucky. People don't stay together very long, like we do, do they?"

He lifted a hand and cupped it on my head. "We're the best," he said automatically. That patting my head thing was a pacifier; he did it to soothe me and keep me from interrupting him. It was a good trick. I leaned into his hand. "It's not like we haven't been tested," I said, testing him.

"Hmm?"

"How long has it been?"

"How long has it been since what?"

"We've been together how many years?"

He sighed and dropped his hand to my shoulder. "Depending on what you mean by 'together,' 15 or 20 years."

"Twenty years," I repeated.

"Did you forget?" His normal voice now was a mixture of disappointment and annoyance. It made me feel I had to be gay to counteract it.

"It's joy," I said cheerily. "Bliss makes it feel like 20 minutes."

"You're making me suspicious."

"Happiness cooks everything fast," I said. "It's a fortune-cookie fact." I made sure I didn't laugh too loud or talk too fast or roll my eyes around like a loose-eyed doll. "I love you," I said. "That's the only problem."

"Calm down. Why is it a problem?"

"Exactly," I said, clapping my hands. "You've got it exactly right."

And then, to reassure him, I got up and washed the dishes. When I was done, I went through the kitchen drawers, straightening them out.

"Did you tell them about the checks?" he asked behind my back, watching me.

"Oh, I found them," I said airily. "It was Bill, the VP, who had them." I reconsidered. "Phil."

He nodded and left. I continued to search. I went through the cabinets, through the canisters and under the sink. I bagged the garbage carefully.

❁ ❁ ❁

I RAN INTO JENNIFER at the coffee machine. "I spoke to the VP," I said. "About you." I felt venomous. "About your attitude. If you don't cause trouble, I won't. If you do cause trouble, I'll win." I stirred an extra sugar in my coffee, to keep my hands from shaking.

"After all these years, you're still a nasty, vicious sneak," she hissed. "After what you did. You'll never change." Her voice choked. She left her coffee on the counter.

I continued to stir mine at my desk. Things weren't going well. That gush of spite from *my* mouth; why would I behave so ungenerously? I couldn't remember anything against her. And she had said I was "still" a sneak. That suggested something, didn't it, about me, about my past? I didn't feel like a sneak. I felt like a kind person being mercilessly pushed and prodded. I would never harm anyone, would I? I would definitely pick up coffee on the outside from now on. I was a kind person, a good person, even though the checks were still missing and I would have to do something about that, all right, I would have to figure out a good explanation. And the sooner the better. If it was a theft, I was giving them time to cash those nine checks, time to cover their tracks.

My misgivings, of course, were that the checks weren't stolen (it would be a relief to find out they were). I was forgetful; I had misplaced them, innocently. Accusations that I was mean and sneaky—well, consider who they came from. Someone who had a grudge against me, exactly what the VP had said, hadn't he? I was the innocent victim of persecution, which was exactly the kind of thing I always did, according to my husband. Though one never "did" one's own victimization, wasn't that true? Could he have meant something else? I went through my drawers again. I had to make out the next payroll soon, but I had to find the checks before then, or at least account for them. I felt a rigidity in my thinking, a rubber band tightening around my thoughts. What if I had been the other woman, after all; what if Jennifer had been betrayed and I had done it?

I was sure I was having an episode, a brain event. There were little flashing sparkles in the air and I was crying. I would have reached for the phone but I'd forgotten the number of someone. So I sat there until it cleared up, and I placed my hand on the keyboard and blinked at the screen. When someone passed the doorway I tapped a key and made a sound of annoyance. I said my name out loud, twice. I said my husband's name. As soon as it was time, I left.

I tried to get into my car but the key wouldn't work. I doublechecked: it was the right key. I tried the passenger side door; it still wouldn't work. What was wrong; why were things always wrong?

"What are you doing?" a man asked. "That's my car."

It was the same color and type as mine, it wasn't my fault. I went down the rows until I found my car. Then I thought about what to do. All these copies of keys wouldn't help if I couldn't find where they connected. I stopped at a store and bought a bottle of blue nail polish and I put a spot of blue next to the car lock. When I got home I put a spot of blue next to the door lock. A very small spot. I put my finger in the dirt and put a small smudge on the other side of the lock. Carlo would complain about the smudge, he would notice the smudge. The blue dot would be invisibly accepted.

Maybe it wasn't an episode at all; I was just feeling pressure. I didn't feel like I'd slid down on the memory slope; I felt no more befuddled, no less bemused. Had my husband been the man in the middle, had he been the one that caused this? He seemed to grit his teeth sometimes, when I got confused. Or maybe I just thought it. I don't remember how we met, it seemed like we'd been together forever, unaccountably bound. Maybe this was the account?

I got home before him. I went through the bedroom, the drawers, under the bed, then I started on the closet. His side first, since it made less sense to be suddenly straightening out his side. When I heard the door slam I called out: "I'm upstairs getting some dry cleaning together. Be down in a sec."

I went to my side, picking first through the shoes, thinking frantically, What would make most sense if they asked me, if he asked me, what details should I offer if they asked me, if he asked me. The questions they would ask me were: What did you do? What are you doing?

Ever since my "events" at least I've thought myself to be decent and caring. At least, I assumed so. Assumed it on a very basic level.

My hands started sweating when I felt a lump in the jacket pocket of the navy blue suit I wore on the day Jennifer complained about the paycheck. Or was it that day? I pulled out an envelope. The checks were separated at their perforations, straight in an orderly pile, neat and shaming.

Had I put them in my pocket because I was distracted by Jennifer? These checks had weight and, I thought, purpose. I was struggling to remember. It seemed to me there was a simple reason why I had them; I had just forgotten what it was. Phil had asked me; or it was someone like Phil, someone with an explanation.

"Are you almost done up there?" Carl called.

"I'm done," I said.

He smiled at me during dinner, Carl did. I tried to remember what he looked like 20 years ago, maybe it would spark something. "Don't we have pictures?" I asked. "When we first met?"

"We've never been much for photos," he said. He was being kind tonight. Maybe he was always kind and I just misinterpreted. "The camera's batteries are always dead when we think of a picture."

"Shouldn't there be someone else," I said. "Someone who takes our picture? A friend? A co-worker?"

"I suppose they keep them, then," he said, not interested.

And why should it suddenly matter whether there are friends somewhere? Someone to talk to; of course. Someone to check with.

❊ ❊ ❊

THE NEXT MORNING, HE said, "Look, do you see how the toast has a curve to it? You should have turned it over before you put butter and jam on it. It's like a bowl, and you put the stuff on the outside of the bowl."

"That's not the problem," I said. "The problem is, why am I making toast for you?"

"You've always said you liked to do it." His tone was aggrieved. Had I hurt him? Was this the right time to hurt him?

Am I a strong or weak woman? Am I resilient? The next day I'm on my way to the mail room when I hear a piece of conversation.

"I wouldn't have guessed, really. She always seemed so nice. And you were married to him?"

I looked in as I passed the room and the voices snapped shut like a box. Two pairs of eyes locked on me. Jennifer and the invoice manager gaped and drew together. I continued past them as if I hadn't heard. So the man was married. Had been married. I concentrated on the sound of my footsteps. I did it to make the ground more certain.

I went to Phil's office. "I have to see you," I said. I couldn't be the kind of person I seemed to be. A sneak, a liar, a stealer of husbands.

"Sit down, sit down," he said, drawing me into a seat and shutting the door.

"I found these checks," I said, taking them out of my pocket. "I found them in my jacket at home. I have no recollection of taking them, but I did notice they were missing. I've been looking for them everywhere."

I handed him the checks and his eyes darted back and forth from them to me. "What does this mean?" he asked in a panic. "Are you a thief? A klepto-something?"

Was I? "I don't know what I am." I tried to say it without emotional content; I wanted to say it simply and purely. Fact of life. We live, we die. I don't know what I am.

"This is a situation," Phil said nervously. "Let me get this straight. You don't remember doing it, you don't know why you did it?" His voice was thin and seemed complaining. I nodded. "This isn't good." He looked me square in the eye. "I think you should go home while I have a chance to figure this out. It's a peculiar thing. We'll just look at the checkbook first, maybe, and a few things." He rubbed his forehead. "And then we'll think about it."

"I'm sorry," I said. "This is scary for me. I think my nerves are shot."

"Of course," he answered, even making a stab at patting my shoulder. "I've known you a long time; if you were going to cheat the company you wouldn't do it like this." He caught himself. "You know what I mean."

We looked at the things in my office. Everything seemed all right, but Phil said we really wouldn't know just by appearances, would we? He idly tapped a key and launched a program. Something caught his eye, or he thought of something to check, because he settled in and started typing. I got my purse and looked in the corner to see if there was a hat or coat hanging. There wasn't. It must be warm out.

"I guess you'll call me," I said. I stood respectfully.

"All right, then," he said, and I left.

I walked down the hall past a couple of women who looked familiar; they stared at me. Maybe they'd heard something about me.

I headed out to the parking lot, passing some more people I didn't really recognize though I smiled and nodded just to be safe. I was feeling relieved, really. It was a terrible task, trying to keep it all in order. The job of it got bigger every day as more and more of it needed to be gathered and held. I had put dots on the ignition lock, on my change purse, on my dominant hand. There was so much still that needed to be identified and classified. So many simple things were becoming elusive. It was a tremendous relief to be relieved, to have someone take a whole corps de ballet of worry away from me. They could do it without me, I wasn't interested, it was getting away from me anyway, slipping through my hands like dead ants.

I found my car, properly marked, waiting where I'd left it; and all the various motions—turn and click and press my foot down blink and turn—they all worked fluidly, automatically. I needed that kind of soothing motion because I still felt a little strange about the checks and the situation and how there seemed to be so many unfamiliar people working in a place I'd gone to every day for so long. It might be science fiction of some kind or something I should have asked about.

It would be good to get home soon and go to bed, I'd like to lie down and dim the lights and listen to a noise machine of the ocean or the rain, something neutrally insistent would be good for me, ushering me into a safe and certain place.

I was thirsty, so I stopped for a pop but I forgot to mark my way back out again and by then it was evening and darkening. Evening up and darkening down. I pulled onto a road that went a long way in a quiet fashion, not much lighting, not much traffic, and I wondered how long it would take, before I got home.

I must have been outside my town on this road, but luckily I was back again though tired, very tired. There was construction all around me, I hadn't noticed it before, it must be new. There were wire fences and large signs of Coming Soon. There were plywood walls and rutted dirts and stripes, some yellow some black. It was a lot of construction, maybe even a construct itself, I remember in school someone talking about constructs and judging by the size this must be one.

But it was dark, despite the flashing lights that were low in places and high in others. Hard going. I was trying to figure if I'd ever been here before, because if I had then I'd know where I was and how far it was from where I should be. It would be nice to situate myself. It would be good to find one point I understood so I could build myself from there. Maybe I could choose this time what I would be and just forget, forget all the jarring things that may or may not be true about me. I can stop being something I don't like; isn't that it? Why continue with a losing proposition. And that woman, Jessica, Jennifer, what was her name something topical—I damaged her and she should just grow past me.

I was so tired that my heart leaped when I finally saw it. A great big yellow sign with a great big black arrow pointing right. And next to the arrow a blue dot. Large enough to be seen at night from a distance, a joy, a blessing, a gift, if I follow the dot I'll be home on the spot.

I just have to concentrate or something. The house is not there right in front of me yet, not in front of my eyes but it's dark except for the occasional yellow blink of the construct eye, the small sweep of the yellow light. The blinks lure me forward, like the sound of the ocean or the neutral fall of rain, it's not unpleasant, it's like being on a ride. And just when my hopes lay low I see another sign and an arrow to the right and a big blue dot.

So the key is always, bear to the right. I understand that this means me, too; I have lost the right way, I was not doing what was right, I wasn't right I was wrong. If I don't go right, I will be left. If I keep to the right I will get home, and all at once there's the yellow sign again with the arrow and the dot and I feel jubilant, really, because it does seem the signs are coming at me in a steady pace, and how can I complain as long as I'm given a sign and it points me, as always, to go right, to be right.

# 7

# ATMOSPHERE

IT WAS DINNERTIME ON the Alzheimer's Floor, and I sat down next to mom, who nodded at me and said, "Alice, I want you to meet Kevin." She motioned to the man to her left at the small table for four.

"Sean," I said, and she winced. I'd been introduced dozens of times. No one ever remembered me.

Sean was fairly deaf and fairly blind. "Who are you?" he asked, his head cocked.

"Alice," I said.

"Ellis?" he asked.

"Alice," I shouted.

"Bessie? If your name is Bessie, I won't talk to you." He picked up his napkin and blew his nose.

The other tablemate sat down, and Sean said, "This is Florence."

Mom shook her head, rolling her eyes. "Not Florence. Her name is Annie."

"It's Eloise," I said.

Mom winced again. After a minute she said, "I wonder how other people are judging me," she said. "What they think of me."

"You know that Robert Burns poem," I said, "*Would some Pow'r the giftie gie us...* I think it's called *To a mouse,* or something."

"That's funny. Writing a poem to a mouse."

"If you wrote one, what would it say?"

"Oh I don't know," she said, smiling. "I don't think I've ever really thought about it. Kevin," she said, calling into Sean's ear, "what if I wrote a poem about a mouse?"

"What's wrong with my mouth?" he said, scraping his hand over his chin. He hadn't shaved in days and he had developed a habit of picking at his whiskers and at the skin on his forehead. He was developing sores. He felt the table for his cutlery. "The service here is terrible," he said.

"Never mind," mother said. She rolled her eyes at me. "What a place," she said. Her eyes looked around the room. "All of them. All of them."

The aide put the food on the table, and Eloise complained that she hadn't heard the specials. Sean felt his plate with his fingers, pushing aside the vegetables.

"What color is this?" he asked, feeling his way through the potatoes.

"They're white," I said. "With soft edges."

"Don't talk to him about food," my mother said. "You should never talk about food."

"That's news to me," I said. "Why is that?"

My mother frowned. She ate the food in the middle and ignored the food on the sides. "There was a girl," my mother said vaguely, frowning. She put her fork down. "I didn't mean a girl. Your father used too much garlic, but now I miss the garlic. You know?"

"I know," I said. "I miss him too."

"This food is tasteless," she said. "I don't know why we came here. Look at all the waitresses at the bar," she said severely, motioning over to the hot plate area, where the aides were still ladling out food.

Sean put down his fork. "Is this all there is?" he asked. He had barely touched his dinner, but he was done.

"This is all there is," I said. "Maybe later there will be ice cream."

My mother's face lit up.

"What did Bessie say?" Sean asked.

"Ice cream," I said, raising my voice. "Ice cream."

"You're a darling," he said. "Will you marry me now or later?"

"I will marry you later," I said. "Unless you get down on your knees and propose."

"Oh, that," he said. "Terrible knees, hurt like hell. And I've already gone down on my knees in another restaurant; you can't do that twice."

I once had someone go down on his knees in a restaurant, too, a week before he left me. And Sean, who sang cabaret years ago, began to hum, and mother joined in, and I also began to sing, and dinner went its way to an imaginary orchestra, with little or no food involved. For one moment we were in a restaurant we knew and loved, with lovers dear and true. The waitresses swept by in glittering outfits, the band played glittering songs, and we all sat back for an instant, caught between what was and what should be.

# 8

# THAT PLACE

KIDNAPPING HER MOTHER MADE Daisy feel terrific. Mildred was belted into the back seat, now that she'd been busted out of that place, and Daisy only wished she could see her brother Boniface's face when they told him that Mildred was gone.

That would take the stride off him.

Boniface always walked into a room as if he was going to plow right past it; when he did stop he swiveled his head and raised his eyebrows, as if to say, You called me in for this?

This time, of course, he'd swing his big head around that place with his eyes popping in surprise and chagrin. And just where did he get that big head? Daisy remembered him as a small boy with a coil of hair and an annoying presence that their mother thought was a joy and a jolt all at once. He got too much of everything, right from the start.

"You just wait, mother," Daisy said, "I'm taking you home and I'm keeping you home. You and me together again, oil and water, salt and pepper." Maybe not the best examples, but her mother didn't understand words anymore.

Daisy switched to the news channel on the radio. Of course it was too soon. She had signed her mother out for lunch and they would probably expect at least two hours for that, so maybe three hours before anyone wondered; maybe four hours before they called Boniface. And indeed they would call Boniface; his name was on all of mother's papers. Although Daisy was the firstborn.

Her car had started up on the fifth try—not as good a sign as starting on the third try, but good enough. She had rapped her knuckles on the wheel lightly and then blown them off—a little mindless ritual that seemed to work well enough, if mindless rituals were ever supposed to actually work. And once she started, she felt like a wild woman, off on a secret mission, a little reckless and bold, bold being pure guesswork since it was the first time she'd tried it.

She allowed a little fantasy of a shootout, just for fun, then got back to reality. "You know where we're going?" she said cheerfully to Mildred once she got her belted into the back seat. "Home! I'm taking you home!" She waited for some recognition, and got nothing. She was used to nothing.

Still, she hoped to hear it on the radio—daughter steals mother from dementia ward. Not ward. Assisted living situation. Not the same ring as ward. She hoped they said ward.

She should probably tell her daughter, Ellabelle, so she wouldn't worry, though when had Ellabelle ever worried?

Ellabelle was a grown woman, married and divorced and on her second marriage, and in some ways sharper and less personal about life than Daisy was. Not less personal; how could she mean less personal; wasn't everyone "personal" about their own lives? But she knew what she meant. Boniface was like that too; he listened to Daisy, blinked, then said No and lost interest in the conversation, if she could call it a conversation. More like a call-and-response from the old days of some church where the churchgoers begged the Lord and the Lord said no.

So maybe Ellabelle was more closely related to Boniface than to Daisy by some sort of random genetic crapshoot, that wouldn't come as a surprise. Boniface got everything; for example, that business of him being on all the legal documents; Boniface attracted power like a magnet sucked up paper clips.

She pulled into the parking lot behind her mother's condo. The car made an extra little noise, and not a pleasant one.

"Okay, now, we're home again," she said in a loud voice, in case the car could hear. "You stay right there." She had to make sure her mother didn't get out first and scoot off—Mildred had a way of heading for cover and disappearing. She was happy to kidnap her mother; she just didn't want to *lose* her mother.

She opened the back door and grabbed her mother's wrist. Mother didn't look at her; her eyes flitted around and around. Maybe this was joy?

The whole kidnapping idea had popped in her head the last time she had visited mother in that place, which wasn't a bad place, filled as her mother's room was with the furniture Boniface had taken from her mother's condo, furniture that Daisy had hoped would be hers. Well, it could be hers—she could take mother and eventually her mother's furniture back home, and in fact, move some of her own stuff in as well. Let's see what Boniface does *then,* she thought. Him and his power of attorney; I doubt the law would say that he can do anything to a daughter taking care of her mother. And if I move her back and stay with her—well, even if I ask to be paid, that's got to be cheaper than whatever he's paying for that place. Good place, but is it better than her having her own home, her own daughter?

❋ ❋ ❋

THEY WENT IN THE front, and Daisy couldn't help but notice that her mother's name wasn't on the mailbox where it used to be. She went on anyway, going to the second floor and putting her key in the lock. Or tried to. The key didn't fit. Keeping one hand on her mother, she went slowly through her keyring. Nope. That was the key.

What had Boniface done? Sold the place already? Without telling her?

She pulled her mother back down the hallway, trying to come up with a different plan. But she didn't have a different plan. Her plan was to bring mother home and stay with her. That was it.

She got Mildred back in the car and belted her in and locked the door. Mother was being no trouble at all; she couldn't be aware of Daisy's failure, could she? Couldn't be let down at Daisy's promises? Or even smug about it all?

Daisy sighed; she had lost that surge of triumph she'd had earlier. She looked at her mother in the rear-view mirror. She was about the size of a child, so small and bony. She remembered being small, and thinking her parents were big. The size thing had gotten all turned around. Mildred was a tiny, senile old lady now.

Well, maybe mother should have a day off from being senile. Couldn't be very exciting in that place, certainly. Where Boniface had landed her and nodded, his work done. She, Daisy, had a better sense of what was due her mother, crazy or not. She would make sure her mother had fun.

She turned the ignition key and got silence. Damn car didn't even *try* to make a sound.

※ ※ ※

"ARE WE TAKING GRANNY back now?" Ellabelle asked. She was driving; Mildred was asleep in the back seat, leaning against a window. She took little itty bitty naps all day long, a habit Daisy would like to have, since she had insomnia; she was often too tired to think straight. No, she thought, I shouldn't say that even to myself. I'm just tired; I think straight. Whereas mother has endless ridiculous energy and doesn't think anymore at all.

"No," Daisy said. "I'm not sure I like her in that place. I'm not sure I'm bringing her back at all." She nodded to herself. Strong words.

"Really," Ellabelle said, not even glancing at Daisy. She had a cold way about her, also mirroring Boniface. And speaking of mirrors, Daisy thought, looking at Ellabelle's profile, her daughter and her brother had similar strong noses. Also curly hair, of course; she'd always wanted Bonny's hair, though not of course now, when it was receding. She was sure that annoyed him.

"I thought it would be nice to take her out for a ride," Daisy said, with a breezy little laugh. Didn't want her daughter to get critical; she often did. True, she had, after all, just come to the rescue after that horrible car failed to start. And Ellabelle hadn't even asked what they were doing there. Daisy said, "Can you believe it? I wanted to stop by granny's home for a visit, and the key was changed. Boniface must have sold the place."

"Sold it? I thought it was a rental," Ellabelle said while Daisy ticked this over in her mind with a little internal groan. "Besides, do you think she would even notice where she was?"

Daisy put on her cheerful voice. "She's stuck in that place all the time and the doors are locked so she never gets out, must feel like a prisoner—"

"She seems all right to me." Ellabelle's eyes flicked to the rear view mirror.

"In what way?" Daisy said, starting to get annoyed

Her daughter cast a quick little look at her then concentrated on driving. "Well, how much does she understand at this point? How much can she want?"

It was a good question, really, and it shouldn't have made Daisy flush, but it did. "That's mean," she said. "Even if her mind's gone—and I'm not saying her mind's *completely* gone—even then, she's still got feelings. She can feel trapped. And forgotten. So she can still want things, Ellabelle."

"But what *specifically* does she want? I mean, how can you know what she wants at this point? She doesn't even talk anymore."

"If you pay attention, you can understand what she's thinking," Daisy said. It sounded weak even as she said it, but there, she couldn't take it back. And it was a silly thing to say after she had dragged her mother back to the condo (or, now that she thought about it, rental), the one Daisy always hoped she'd somehow inherit, though Boniface no doubt was listed in the will—

Daisy twisted a little to look at the back seat. Her mother's eyes were open and staring at her. "Sweet as jam," she said in a bright voice. "Have a nice nap, mother?"

"What did she say?" Ellabelle mock-whispered in an equally loud voice.

❖ ❖ ❖

HER MOTHER HAD STOPPED talking last year. It had been a gradual thing, and in the end, before she gave up communicating altogether, she would point at objects if she wanted them. Water. Shoes. The door. Daisy took away her knives, one by one, because she was afraid one day her mother would point at a knife. What would that mean?

"Funny," Boniface had said. "All her knives are missing. Do you think the aide is stealing knives?" Because Boniface brought in aides, a little at a time, to help her mother out.

"I think the aides are stealing knives," Daisy had said, her face getting red as Bonny's eyes stayed on her.

Which probably explained why Bonny showed up at Daisy's apartment the next week, unannounced. Daisy had been meaning to clean, but cleaning implied optimism, didn't it, that someone would come, that things would be better? Bonny should have called first. Daisy almost didn't answer the door—still in a bathrobe, her hair stringy, clothes and paper in piles around the place—but she did, and there was Bonny.

"May I come in?" he asked, looking over her shoulder. At the mess, of course.

She hesitated. Should she ask him to stay outside for 10 minutes or 10 hours while she got herself together? He was her brother. She stepped back. "Of course, come in," she said, clutching her robe defiantly, as if he cared. He stood in the living room, his head scanning. Was he wondering whether he would consider sitting down on this furniture? She felt a sudden urge to flee and said she had to dress, she'd be right back, make himself at home.

She ripped through her closet and found a decent shirt, a decent pair of slacks. She put on shoes, she swiped at her hair and pulled it back, put on a touch of lipstick (not too much, she didn't want him to think she was going to any trouble for him), and went back to find her brother standing in the kitchen, one of her mother's knives in his hand.

"I found this," he said, his eyebrows raised. Of course they were raised. It wasn't even a clean knife, he'd taken it from the counter where it lay near some smeared cheese from the night before.

"The aide didn't take it," he said, and placed the knife in the sink.

What could Daisy do but stand there with her mouth open, her face getting hotter and hotter as Bonny watched. "She could have," she said faintly. "It's not the same as if I was living there, for instance," she trailed off. "And got paid for it." She stood there, her heart muttering in her chest.

He said nothing.

"You must think I'm crazy," she said finally.

"I don't think you're crazy," he said, weighing out each word. "I just think you're wrong." He headed for the door, and left without another word. What had he come for? Was that his goal—just to put her in her place?

She didn't even imagine there was a way to make this better. She'd talked to Bonny before when he'd caught her at something silly, and all it did was make her aware of how much he enjoyed her failures.

For years she had hoped to get back at him. For years. She wanted one moment of triumph, one moment when she could jolt him out of his rightness, his complacency, his contempt, his success and his power.

Because Bonny could afford to get mother some aides, he had a decent job and access to mother's money. Daisy was too poor to make the offer, too poor to bring the helpful gadgets Bonny brought her, or the plush slippers. Being poor put Daisy at a moral disadvantage. And she knew perfectly well that she'd taken the knives because they were much better knives than she had at home, a miserable little apartment compared to the condo where her mother lived. Her mother even had a spot for her car, which just sat in its spot day after day while Daisy had to find a way to patch her own car up, bargaining for the minimum repairs at the service station, crossing her fingers when she turned the ignition key. And then, searching for a parking spot on the street, and hoping she wouldn't get ticketed when the car wouldn't start. And the crushing thing was—she didn't feel that she could actually *say* she was broke; what would her daughter think of her; what would Boniface think of her? Of course they knew she wasn't rich, but if they knew the numbing dailiness of wondering how to pay for things; no, that would confirm something she was convinced they suspected about her. You couldn't respect someone who was always broke.

So she'd let things get too far, everywhere. Before Boniface had moved Mildred, she'd tried sleeping on Mildred's sofa so Boniface would suggest she move in with mother, which would have meant she could give up paying rent in that miserable little place on Forum Street, and maybe get some kind of salary to boot. But it had been a failure; the aide had complained to Boniface, and Boniface liked the aide.

❖ ❖ ❖

"WHERE ARE WE DRIVING, by the way, or do I just keep going and see where I land?"

"To the zoo. Not so much the zoo as the playground area. I used to love it as a child. Mother did, too. And the carousel! She would stand beside me, tall as a tree, while I rode on a lion. She was a young woman, I realize." She thought for a moment. "Why, really, probably not much more than your age." Silence again. "How bizarre is time. Not bizarre. Bitter. Time is bitter." She turned to look at her mother in the rear seat. She had fallen asleep again, her wrists facing up, a particularly vulnerable thing, Daisy thought, and perhaps it meant her mother trusted her without question, which made her suddenly feel fragile, as if she weren't trustworthy and would screw this up somehow. No doubt that was how Boniface felt about her, always. She lifted her head up. She had always had to fight against her own impression of Bonny's impression of her. We get trapped by imagining how others think of us, she decided. The only freedom was not to ever think of them thinking at all.

"That looks like a parking spot," Ellabelle said.

Naturally. Some people *always* found parking spots, and those people were Boniface and Ellabelle. When you didn't have luck, you didn't have it in a lot of unimportant ways, though avoiding parking tickets was a pretty important way, of course.

Daisy turned to her mother in the back seat, who already was awake and had her hand on the door. "Mother? We're at the zoo. Remember? Birds and cats and seals and oh I don't know what else—the carousel? Remember you always took me on the carousel?"

Mildred wouldn't meet her eye; nothing new there. She flicked the handle for the windows, probably thinking it was the door. Daisy told her daughter not to unlock the door until she had gotten out and could stand next to it when her mother opened it. Mildred could be surprisingly smart when she chose.

Successfully done. "Good," she breathed as her mother climbed out, but once she straightened up she dropped her arm and Mildred was off and running.

"Hey!" Ellabelle shouted, cell phone in hand.

"I'll catch her and wait for you," Daisy yelled back over her shoulder. Who was Ellabelle phoning? It wouldn't be Boniface, would it? Daisy's day was getting rough.

Mildred was amazing, 89, skinny as a chopstick and a lot faster than Daisy, so she relied on desperate measures. "Would you like an ice cream?" she yelled, and her mother slowed down. She was fond of ice cream. "I'll get you an ice cream!" Daisy yelled again. Her mother's head had begun to turn, searching for the ice cream truck no doubt (though other more important things had vanished from her mother's brain, ice cream stayed).

When Daisy caught up with her, Mildred was pointing at a picture on the cart. "We'll have that—coconut is it?—good choice, mother," Daisy babbled, looking at the price (almost five dollars for an ice cream, could it be possible?), then grimly pulled a small change purse from her jacket pocket and counted the money out. She'd have to get Ellabelle to pay for zoo admission, somehow, though she had invited everyone and by rights she should pay. And she would pay if she had more money, but how would she get through the week if everything was gone so quickly? She thought for a moment that it had been stupid to do this, come here, but she snapped it out of her mind. She couldn't falter so quickly; she must borrow some money from Ellabelle, not just admission, some real money, or it would all go wrong.

There was Ellabelle now, tucking her cell phone into her purse.

"She sure likes ice cream," Ellabelle said.

"She always refused to eat it, said she didn't want to get fat," Daisy said, nodding. "She never let herself have anything she liked. Built character. Built moral fiber. She was mean to herself," she said suddenly, thoughtfully.

Mildred stopped before she was finished with the ice cream and dropped it on a bench. Daisy got it, wiped the bench, and threw the cone out. She looked around and saw that Mildred was watching a dog on a leash. She took her mother by the elbow and bent her head to meet her mother's head.

"Ellabelle," she cried, "what do you see? Are the two of us twins?"

"You're a card, ma," Ellabelle said patiently. "Good for a riot."

"Let's go to the zoo," Daisy said, taking her mother's arm. She was docile today, at least, no fighting or silent crying. That silent crying thing was awful. She just scrunched up her face, made no sounds at all as tears and snot rolled down to fall on her chest. Tears and snot! Daisy had to run for tissues, clean her up. She couldn't get over it: tears and snot! Her mother, the baby.

Although she knew well enough that this was a disease, this wasting away of her mother's mind, still it had sunk in further at different times. Helping her mother to dress—her nude mother, who undressed herself at times and seemed puzzled by the lack of clothes. Her prudish mother! She was horrified on the old lady's behalf! But also—why couldn't her mother have protected her from this? Why in the world was she forced to see such things, to clean up (as she had) after her mother's toilet "accidents" (she bet Bonny never did; he knew when to walk away). This woman who had loomed over her life monumentally—whose words had formed her daily actions in childhood, who had influenced her against all reason in adulthood—this woman, reduced to this!

They were at the gate. "Oh, I've got to hold on to mother," Daisy said to Ellabelle. "Can you just get this?" Let her pay for the admissions. "Remember, granny's a senior." She scooted through, turned just enough to see Ellabelle digging in her pocket. She held on to Mildred for dear life: she had the consistency of a chicken wing, all saggy bones.

"I said you were a senior, too," Ellabelle said, holding her head down as she handed the tickets over. Was that a smile on her face? A smile of satisfaction? Was she thinking (as Daisy couldn't help but think) that someday her own mother would be this old, odd creature and she would bring her out on a sunny day as a special treat?

Daisy looked at her daughter and saw her smile back. No, her daughter was kind. A little rough, maybe, a little predisposed to argue and disagree with her (as most people were, she'd found), but at her heart, good. She smiled back.

Her mother kept moving forward. She was a stick of an engine, driven any which way, she didn't have a pattern. Well, maybe I don't have a pattern, either, Daisy thought, then shrugged the thought away. She had plans, she had a goal. A few goals. Like today, she was planning on getting Ellabelle to lend her some money, now that Mildred's condo had turned into an apartment. It hadn't worked out, but it was still an example of a goal. Maybe she should rely on Ellabelle more; take her into her confidence. Wouldn't Ellabelle back her up? A daughter back up her mother? How hard was that?

They'd reached the carousel. "Alley-oop," she said, grabbing her mother's elbow and helping her up onto the moving platform. Mildred pointed at one of the horses, though Daisy had hoped to place her on one of the benches. Her mother pulled her, there was no turning aside, so she might as well, no? Might as well. Her mother was on the horse. Other mothers—and a few fathers—helped their small children up, pointedly not looking at Mildred, though the children did. Fascinated them, no doubt: was Mildred a child or an adult? Hard to say.

❄ ❄ ❄

AT LEAST SHE WAS out of that residence Boniface had put her in. Boniface, the second-born, the golden boy (apparently), with the money and the say-so. Let him look around that place he'd put her in and frown and call for an aide or go straight to the director and demand—demand— that something be done.

"What do we do after this?" Ellabelle asked, coming up next to them on the carousel. A man was making his way through the horses and carts, collecting tickets. "You can't stand," he said to them. "Safety. You have to sit."

"But we have to keep an eye on her," Daisy said. "My mother. She is, you know," she dropped her voice and said, "senile. Demented. Can't be trusted."

"Sit or get off," he said, moving on.

"I'll get off," Ellabelle said. "I get dizzy anyway. Why don't you just take the horse next to her? Close enough."

So Daisy did, as Ellabelle got off just before the carousel started. And to be honest, it was fun pretending to be a kid pretending to be on a real horse. She said, out loud, "Whee!" to catch her mother's eye, but Mildred was holding on with two hands and staring straight ahead. Was she having fun? Was fun a possibility? Why wouldn't she talk or interact in any way? It was all guesswork, having to figure out what to do with her. But it was safe to say she wasn't happy in that place, that horrible place, though it was clean enough and smelled all right. But the false smiles, the deadening waits for something to happen, it drove Daisy crazy and if you were already crazy it must drive you even further, over the edge, straight down to silence (though of course she was silent before; but maybe the demented can see the future?).

So she, Daisy, was a champion, taking her mother away from all that. Hard to say what that would mean in the long run, but for now it was an escape, wild outlawhood. She got a thrill whenever she thought of it, how annoyed Boniface would be, how maybe she could get her mother to talk again—now wouldn't that just kill Boniface if he came charging in at some point, ready to grab Mildred and take her back to that place, raising his eyebrows even higher than normal at Daisy, icy with annoyance— wouldn't it be terrific if her mother then said, "Boniface, shut up. Daisy is right."

Daisy is right! A phrase she's longed to hear all her life.

She smiled to herself and looked at her mother, who was looking at her, looking at her with something like a sharp look of intelligence. The look made Daisy freeze: her mother, in a shaft of sunlight, looking for a moment like her old self, ready to say something smart, looking aware and intelligent.

And then Mildred was off. She'd been standing next to her horse, not sitting on it; perhaps that's what had caused Daisy to look up. Daisy was startled, but acted as quickly as she could, climbing off her horse, getting the strap of her bag hooked on it, a precious second or two spent correcting that. She shouted "Ellabelle!" and then "Mother!," stumbling off the carousel, looking madly around for her mother, her daughter.

In a way it was wonderful.

She knew she couldn't let her mother get away—how would she explain?—so she took off at a run, clutching her flying clothes, lifting her chin. When was the last time she'd run, really? Full-out, not caring how she looked or who she crashed into? And when was the last time she filled her lungs and shouted? "Mother! Wait! Stop that little old lady!" Of course it was bad, of course she'd get in trouble, she always got in trouble, it's why she tucked herself in and tried to be unobtrusive; but this was cinematic and she was sure to find her mother—her mother was *old*, goddammit, she'd be bound to get tired and stop soon, wouldn't she?

Behind her, she heard Ellabelle yelling, "Mom! Wait! What's going on?"

People were getting out of her way, staring, pointing, moving their strollers and bikes and what not, pushed aside by Daisy's mad rush, she felt herself starting a wind (how many knots would that be?), but she was getting a stitch in her side and she was gasping. How soon! How soon it all collapsed! She was gasping, her mother nowhere in sight, and here was Ellabelle gaining on her, calling, "Where is granny? What happened? Where *is* she?" as if Daisy was holding out on her.

Tears sprang to her eyes, but she bent over, gulping down air, intent on restoring whatever oxygen loss had tilted her world upside down. Where was her mother? How could she know? All she knew was that she had to run again, and she did, right before Ellabelle could actually place the hand she was extending towards her on her, and once again she shouted, "Mother!" and felt the glory of other people's eyes on her, shying away from her, what power she felt, more than she'd ever had, and then, she rounded the corner, where the pretzel seller met up with the hot dog seller, and just beyond them where the path turned, there was traffic and danger. Her mother had slowed down for a moment (pretzel? hot dog?) and Daisy shot herself forward, faster, with no reserves left, the last bit of air squeezed out behind her, coming up to grab her mother's arm, unable to speak, not able to slow down either, so that between her speed and her mother's tensed intention to get away, they spun around and landed on the grass, toppling over, rolling around on whatever was on the grass—

acorns, popsicle sticks, things one shouldn't see—rolling as if they were kids, the two of them two generations not acting their age. She could hear Boniface shouting, "Stop them! Stop those two!" As if he were the cop of me, Daisy thought, glad to note that no one here thought enough of Boniface to do a thing. I should come here more often, she thought, as Boniface continued to shout and be ignored, shout and be ignored.

And the two of them, out of breath, stopped rolling altogether, panting. Daisy was laughing, a good belly of a laugh, not something she'd done since she was a kid, and she was happy to hear her mother laugh too, until at once it struck her that her mother no longer laughed, it was part of her silence, and she jumped to her feet and started shouting and waving, "She's laughing, Boniface! Laughing!" and she pointed at mother and pointed at herself and said, "I did it Bonny, I made her laugh and you couldn't do it if you stood on your head and barked like a poodle, who's the best kid yet?" (Was she really saying it, shouldn't she shut up before her mouth dug a hole that not even Bonny could get her out of?) Oh look, how Ellabelle had her hand on Bonny's arm, trying to smooth down his great red face, no doubt, was that what apoplexy looked like? And it was no surprise, her daughter's loyalties ran to Bonny, she'd always known, really, the two of them lived alike, and those glimpses of Ellabelle putting away her cell phone really only meant that she was giving Bonny their locations, not a new betrayal, though it hurt every time.

Bonny and Ellabelle lifted Mildred up and dusted her off. Daisy stood by, annoyed a little at how she was being ignored until she noticed how the two of them kept flicking their eyes at her. And then, eyes on her, hands on mother, they wandered off back towards Ellabelle's car (no doubt Bonny had found a space right in front of her) as children shrieked and the sun shone imperturbably. Of course she knew that, no matter how her heart smarted and her love got shredded, the one true thing was that those two had their eyes on *her* and it was a kind of love, wasn't it, to be unable to let go of those who tormented you, as she no doubt tormented them, as they indeed tormented her. Wasn't it love when the same people could both ignore you and grab every ounce of you, like a mad kind of moon yanking up the tides?

Like her mother, she thought. Who pulls more strongly now that she's left us all behind. Daisy dusted off her threadbare clothes and turned to follow the three who made up life for her—Mildred, Bonny, and Ellabelle.

She hurried to keep up with them, and as she got closer, Mildred let go of Ellabelle and held her hand out, and Daisy took it. She could have reached out to nothing, Daisy thought, but she reached out to me. There's something there for sure, she told herself. Something was left in Mildred that reached out for her. Daisy took her hand and felt the day was good, maybe only for this minute, but this minute had its own charm. "You're a laugh riot, mother," she said affectionately and grinned, swinging her mother's arm. If only her mother could grin right back at her; if only she could have that.

"I've changed my mind," Boniface said, all the way at the other end of the line of linked hands, Daisy to Mildred to Ellabelle to Boniface. "You aren't *wrong*," he said. "You're crazy."

Daisy waited to see if there was anything else.

"Ah well," he added, shrugging gracefully. "I just can't tell if you were born crazy or if you took it on as your duty. The two of you—the two of you—loopy as sunshine." He nodded at his phrase, feeling it said it all. "Loopy as sunshine."

Whatever the hell *that* meant, Daisy thought, but it sounded nice and friendly in an odd sort of way, and they walked in links up the small hills and down the small vales, with the sound of the crowds around them, everything very ordinary, and they were ordinary too, just a family out for the day, and heading back home now, to that place.

# 9

# CORA

"WHO ARE YOU?" HER mother asked.

"I'm your daughter, Alice."

"I know that. But I mean, who are you?" Her mother's eyes locked onto hers; she was clutching Alice's eyes. What did she mean, then?

"I love you," Alice said. "Don't you know that?"

"But who are you?"

"Alice."

"How did you find me? How did you know where to look?"

"I'll always find you. Wherever you are, I'll find you." Her mother looked a little easier at that. She always thought she was in prison now, trapped somewhere, for a crime she couldn't remember. She felt, sometimes, that the charges were false. At other times the charges didn't matter; it was just the prison aspect that bothered her. The strange people, the rules, the being told what to do. Alice took her mother's hand. "You're my mother," she said. "Isn't that terrific? To have a daughter like me?" She grinned and winked.

"All my daughters are wonderful," her mother said.

"All of them?" Alice wondered and paused. "How many do you have?"

Her mother's focus shifted to a point beyond Alice's shoulder. "Oh, you know," she said, troubled.

"Of course. All of us."

Just then Cora came in, the brightest aide on the floor. "Why look at you!" Cora cried. "You're looking all bright today. How you feeling?"

Her mother's face lit up. "My daughter," she said confidentially to Alice. "Lovely girl."

Alice looked at Cora. The woman had a pleasant, smiling face. She moved around the room, setting up the lunch tray, putting the teabag in the hot water, unwrapping cutlery. Maybe that was it—the motions of the home, preparing a meal. Maybe that made her seem like a daughter. Alice told herself to fight the flare of dislike; she knew it was jealousy.

She patted her mother's hand. "Remember that time you came to visit and we went to the auction and you met an old friend?"

"That was Cora," her mother said.

Alice took this in. "The old friend?"

"I went to visit Cora." Her mother's face looked relaxed as she followed Cora's movements.

"Don't mind that," Cora said to Alice, not worrying about what she said in front of her mother. "I'm everything to everybody. Comes with the territory."

"That was me," Alice said to her mother. "You came to visit me and we went to an auction and you met a friend you hadn't seen in 20 years. That was remarkable, wasn't it? How out of the blue you can be surprised like that. It was lovely."

"It was lovely," her mother said, frowning. "Did you come with us?"

She cast her eyes at Cora, who said, "I wasn't there; your daughter Alice was there."

"Alice?" her mother said uncertainly.

Alice looked at Cora. Things were being stolen away, bit by bit. Her mother got lost for a while, and then she found her footing and came back. But there were things that got dropped by the roadway; things that were valuable to her and, perhaps, more valuable to Alice.

And Cora was getting them.

"When I was a little girl," Alice said, "you made me a doll from bits and pieces of fabric. A rag doll. The most beautiful doll ever."

"I don't remember."

"Very traditional. Buttons for eyes. Yarn for hair."

"I don't remember."

"I still have it. I'll bring it next time. Maybe that will, that will strike a chord!" She raised her hands up, as if she had just finished a keyboard flourish.

Her mother raised her hands up automatically, mimicking the flourish.

"You play piano," Alice reminded her.

"It's been a while," her mother agreed. "I wanted to play more than I did play."

You remember *that*, Alice thought bitterly. She watched as Cora left the room, saying a merry "See you later!"

Her mother nearly sat up, her mouth agape. "Cora," she whispered.

Alice brought the doll the next time she came. Her mother barely woke that day; she opened her eyes, smiled a little and said Hello then closed her eyes again. Alice tried to show her the doll, tried to tell her what she'd been doing, but her mother's eyes when she opened them, were dull and disinterested.

Alice went in search of Cora.

"Oh yes," Cora said. "She had a restless night, I heard about it. Yelled all night for Eleanor; who's Eleanor?"

"I don't know anyone named Eleanor."

"Your mother does, I guess."

"I don't think so."

Cora looked at her appraisingly. "Could be. Could just be a name she heard and it stuck in her mind. That's what happens. Just what comes into her head now."

"She thinks you're her daughter," Alice blurted out. She didn't say it in a nice way, either.

Cora moved slowly, picking something up and putting it down. Alice didn't see what it was; her eyes were watching Cora's face.

"Well," Cora said, finally. "I'm around a lot and I'm taking care of her. She thinks that means a daughter."

"I come almost every day." Alice heard her own voice being petulant; who would want a daughter with a petulant voice? Cora's voice was sweet and giving.

"She talks about you when you're not here, though," Cora said. "She's always asking me when is Alice coming, and I remind her. I say you just hold on, Alice will be here."

"But she doesn't recognize me," Alice said, surprised. "She doesn't know who I am."

"Maybe not when you're here. She's thinking of another Alice, maybe."

"Another Alice?"

"A little girl, maybe. It's hard to know what she's thinking, what part she remembers. But yes, a little girl. She saved some candy the other day— just a piece of chocolate—she saved it for Alice."

Alice thought about this carefully. She was too old to be the daughter her mother remembered; not a comforting thing. There was another Alice in her mother's mind, crowding out the true Alice. So Cora wasn't the one she should be jealous of. She wasn't sure how Cora fitted in, but it was this younger version of herself who kept kicking her out of the picture. She sighed, closed her eyes briefly, it was more than she could handle for the day. She would have to think how she would become the true Alice in her mother's mind, before it was too late, before the final farewell.

Perhaps, for that, she needed to connect with what her mother was, as well, with the mother she saw now, who wasn't the mother in her head either.

She nodded to Cora. "So where's that candy my mother saved for me?"

"Oh, sorry," Cora said. "I ate it."

# 10

# THE TERRIBLE JOURNEY

An enormous wave," Jubilee said. "I saw it. Taller than the ship itself, it ran right over the other side of the ship. People swept away. Horrible." Jubilee's face was anxious, but not as anxious as Clarice thought she would be if *she'd* seen it. They were sitting together in Jubilee's rooms on the Memory Ward.

"No one could do anything?'" Clarice asked tentatively. She patted her sister's hand. Jubilee wore a jade green knit top and houndstooth stretch trousers. Her hair was gray and cut short, and she'd put on a little weight in the past few years, but she still seemed vigorous; she was still Jubilee. But her face never looked as relaxed as it once did.

"There was wind for a minute but then it all died down. I was wearing a skirt and it whipped around my thighs so that I had to hold it down because there was a crowd of men all staring out the windows of the main deck, all of them grinning at me."

"You've always been something to look at," Clarice said. She was looking for a place where she could change the story, change her sister's latest delusion. All her delusions were dreadful.

"Well, I didn't want to go in, with them there, but I didn't want to stay on deck. I could see another wave, and I was frightened. I wondered if I would die this way, very slightly, you know, like a stone dropped in water."

"I'm so glad you got away," Clarice said, rubbing her sister's hand. She always took her sister's hand when she told her stories, because the stories were always bad.

"I'm still frightened. What if it happens again? No one can tell me about those waves, I ask them and they look at me funny, like they know something I don't know. I think they wanted me to be swept away, gone overboard, wanted it to look like an accident. But can they *make* waves like that, do you think?" Her voice was getting lower, she was hunkering down between her shoulders.

"Waves that high?" Clarice tilted her head to signal that she was thinking it over. "Do you think so?"

"They were like mountains. It was the most incredible thing. And those people staring at me, laughing at me! They wanted me dead. They wanted to watch me die!" Her face started to scrunch up the way it did these days, pulled into the center—lips, eyes, eyebrows all pulled together around her mouth, tight and about to burst.

"Who are they?" Clarice asked quickly, getting her sister to look at the details, always a good thing to keep her away from the awful mysteries swallowing her up.

"Some of them are familiar. I know who they are. That man from down the street—Gerry Darr, I never liked him—he's there, looking out the window. He has a mustache now. Next to him is my great-uncle, Selmer, I don't know why. He pinched me once, maybe he meant to hurt me."

Clarice didn't remember a great-uncle Selmer. But this was Jubilee's story. "I don't trust men who pinch," she said.

Jubilee nodded gratefully. "You know what the weird thing is—they all looked a little alike. I mean, you see them all lined up at the windows like that, and they're all the same height and they have the same kind of nose and chin. I think there's something going on with that."

"I want to check that out," Clarice said. "I want to get to the bottom of it. What else did you notice about them?"

Jubilee sat back, suddenly tired. "They're everywhere," she said. "I don't want to go back in because they're all in there. And out there," she waved vaguely, "all those waves. All those terrible waves. I can hear them screaming even now."

"Who? Who's screaming?"

"The ones who got washed overboard. That's what they want: they want me to go overboard too." She began to cry. "What can I do? What have I done?"

❖ ❖ ❖

Suddenly Jubilee said, "Clarice! We're getting old!" She looked at Jubilee in shock, then tried to hold it back, shutting her mouth and widening her eyes.

"We're old," Clarice agreed. She tried to smile reassuringly. Of course they were getting old. How could anyone forget that? "How old do you think we are?"

Jubilee's eyes flicked over Clarice's face, her hair, her clothes. "I'm thirty—"

Clarice shook her head.

"Forty?"

"You're sixty-four," Clarice said. "I'm sixty-six."

Jubilee drew in a breath. "No," she said, shocked. "No! But I don't feel that way. I don't feel so old."

"You never see yourself here," Clarice said, thinking aloud. "You don't have a good mirror and you never look at yourself. Why, you could be a teenager and you wouldn't know!" She was gently trying to mock her sister, whose face was running through emotions: shock, dismay, disgust, horror—emotions Clarice was trying not to notice because they made her feel awful. They were old; it was over.

Jubilee looked up hopefully at the word *teenager* but her gaze fell on Clarice's hair, and she pursed her lips in disapproval. "Really, Clarice, I know we're old; I've always known it." But she looked away and was silent after that; her fingers rippling on her lap, as if constantly moving abacus beads, counting again and again.

A few days later, Clarice brought her a full-length mirror. She propped it in the corner of the living room, opposite the door, until she sat down and saw her own reflection; it was too annoying seeing every move mirrored like that. She moved it into the small bedroom, in a spot where it wouldn't be, she thought, too intrusive—next to the dresser, a natural spot, if a little crowded.

Jubilee now lived on Staten Island; Clarice lived in downtown Brooklyn. Clarice visited a few times a week, driving there when she wanted to take Jubilee somewhere—doctors, dinner out—or taking the train to the ferry, the ferry to the railway, and walking to the residence. Some days she needed the extra travel time to deal with the reluctance that built up in her heart. Jubilee wearied her as she was; she wanted her sister back.

Jubilee's husband had left the previous year, paying for the residence regularly, but Clarice worried that one day those checks would disappear as he had, and she would have to figure out what to do with Jubilee. Her husband had disappeared; his money might disappear; she was disappearing. Once, Clarice had made it all the way to the residence and then turned around, unable to bear it that day.

The mirror didn't get mentioned for days and days, and Clarice thought it was working, keeping her sister attached to the present, until the day she let herself in and heard voices from Jubilee's bedroom.

"Jube, it's me: Clarice," she called, wondering if one of the aides was with her.

"Oh, come in, come in," Jubilee called, her voice high in happiness, lifted up with joy. "Come see who's here!"

Clarice moved to the bedroom and saw Jubilee on a folding chair, pulled up close to the mirror, leaning in towards it. "It's Granny," she said, "come in, come in, I can't believe she's here! It's been so long!" And she turned back to the mirror, waving happily. Granny waved back, smiling, happy as could be. "We were talking about when the car broke down and the police officer came on his horse to rescue us? Remember that?"

Clarice stood where she was, processing it all. Jubilee had brought in the cafe table from the living room, and two folding chairs. She was sitting next to the mirror, twisted towards it. She turned away from Clarice and smiled fondly at her own image. "Granny admitted she made the whole thing up. It was her neighbor who came as the police officer, wasn't it? That man down the street, the one with the mustache and the flat hat?" She listened. "Porkpie hat." She turned to Clarice. "Come sit with us. I'm having a wonderful time. She brought cookies." She motioned toward a box of cookies on the table. It was the box Clarice had brought two days before.

Well, what should she do? She stood to the side, wondering if the illusion would be broken if she appeared in the mirror as well. If Jubilee saw Clarice twice—in the room, and in the mirror—would it ruin everything for Jubilee? Her sister looked so wonderfully happy.

"You two talk," Clarice said abruptly. "I had a long chat with Granny last night, and besides, I've got a few things to do." She turned and sat in the living room until it was time to leave. Jubilee's excited voice spilled out from the bedroom, laughing confidentially.

❀ ❀ ❀

"HOW DID YOU FIND me?" Jubilee cried out when she saw Clarice open the door. "How did you know where to look?"

"Of course I'd find you," Clarice said. "I'll always find you, wherever you are. That's what sisters are for." She took her coat off and sat down on the loveseat next to her sister's chair. Jubilee had sprained her ankle the day before and it was still sore. She had her feet up on a footstool. She was very agitated. "Are you all right?" Clarice said. "Tell me what's been happening."

"The guards were out there earlier," Jubilee whispered. "They took some people away while we were all eating. I don't know where they took them. I saw it out the window. I don't know what will happen to them. I won't go near the window again; they might see me and take me away too." Her eyes darted around. She was talking about the residential dining room, which doubled as an activities area. Some of the people at the home never moved, sitting slumped in their chairs. Others never stopped moving. Aides came and went, too, and since some of the residents were male, there were male aides as well. Clarice assumed Jubilee had noticed aides escorting people to their rooms, or to the bathroom, or to some other activity. All her sister had understood was that they'd been taken away, one by one. But what window did Jubilee mean? Her window didn't look out to the windows of the dining room.

It was one of Clarice's reluctant days, and it was cruel, in a way, that she couldn't even allow herself to say she was having a bad day; her sister's day was always worse.

"Can you cover up the window?' Jubilee whispered to Clarice. "Anyone can see right in; those curtains aren't thick enough. They keep walking back and forth, looking this way. I'm afraid someone will come right up to the window and look through the curtains and see me. Cover the windows, Clarice!" Her voice was shaking. Her eyes were bright and moist.

They were on the fourth floor, but Clarice found a thick dark throw and draped it over the curtain rod, over the white curtain that Jubilee found inadequate. Sometimes just moving her worked, but sometimes Jubilee wouldn't let go of an obsession, and this seemed like one.

"They can't see you now," she told Jubilee, whose eyes closed in relief. She seemed frozen there, still afraid, and after a minute of watching, Clarice sat down on the sofa, leaned over, and put her hand on Jubilee's.

Jubilee kept her eyes hard shut. "Who is that?" she whispered. "Who is that with my hand?"

❊ ❊ ❊

JUBILEE LOOKED BRIGHT AND alert. It was a good day, one of her good days. Clarice could feel the knots in her neck loosen. Jubilee had brushed her hair, had pulled it back off her face with clips at either side. She had on some makeup. She was straightening out a small pile of cards and envelopes on the coffee table, some old newspapers on the couch. She put the box of cookies Clarice had brought weeks earlier on a plate. "Here, have some cookies. They're very nice. I think that man down the street brought them."

"What man down the street?"

"I can't remember his name. Vaguely German or French. Foreign, but not too foreign. He always wants to talk to me. Gerry Darr? Is that it? I think he's got a little crush." She laughed ruefully. "I'm not sure he's all there, you know?' She raised her eyebrows significantly.

"Perhaps not."

"But if he *is* all there, he's not an unattractive man. I'm thinking of inviting him in for coffee. Not a drink, not till I know if his mentis is compos. But he goes away a lot, always flying off somewhere." She gave a little laugh. "What's new with you? Are you seeing anyone?"

"I haven't seen anyone in years."

Jubilee stopped her restless movement and looked closer at her sister. "My god, Clarice, what happened to you? You look so old."

"I'm sixty-six, Jubilee."

"You're not! Why that would make me—" She tried hard to think. "I don't know. What does that make me? I think I'm thirty, thirty-one?"

"You're two years younger than I am."

"I'm not thirty-one, then. Twenty-nine? That makes more sense." Her voice was getting broken, however. Her eyes were getting that terrified look. "You're getting old, Jubilee," she said again, and burst into tears.

❊ ❊ ❊

"I THINK WE'VE GONE past our stop," Jubilee said with agitation. "I don't recognize anything now. None of this looks familiar." They were in Jubilee's living room and she was sitting on her loveseat, looking to her right, out the window. She had forgotten about the men who could look into her window and take her away; the curtains were open.

Clarice couldn't figure out what made her think of a subway; what about the room suggested any of that, other than the fact that she was sitting parallel to a window?

"Where is it going? Where is this train going? It's going too fast, Clarice. There's something terribly wrong. Can you make it stop? Pull the cord, pull the emergency cord. We're going to crash horribly, we'll go off the tracks and then what will happen to us?" She began to cry.

Clarice grabbed her sister's hands and held them clenched together. "This isn't a train," she said carefully. "You're at home. You're in your room. Look around. Do you see that refrigerator, that sink? You have a kitchenette here in your apartment. We're sitting in your living room. I'm on your sofa. You can see your bookcases across from us. There's a TV on top of the bookcase. See? If we were on a train, everything would be shaking, wouldn't it? Look out the window, there. Is it all moving by us? It isn't. Look at the pictures on the wall. They're the pictures you've had for years, the ones you like the most. Remember?" She followed Jubilee's eyes around the room, waiting for each item to register. Her sister began to calm down, her breath slowed, her face relaxed slowly.

"This is my place," she said at last. "I'm back. Thank you." She lifted her sister's hands and kissed them.

❃ ❃ ❃

CLARICE FOUND HER SISTER in the dining room again; all the residents were still sitting at their tables. A few of them were nodding off. The mood in the room was depressed. Clarice could feel it even from the aides; they must have had a rough morning. They, too, got exhausted.

"Take me away from here!" Jubilee cried when she saw her sister. Clarice took her by the hand, nodding at the aides who watched her without a smile. She walked her sister down the hallways, carpeted, wallpapered, with vignettes (a wedding dress on a coat rack; a jigsaw puzzle on a small table; an old record player), past the closed doors of the other residents, each with the resident's photo and name, turning down the final hallway to Jubilee's room. A little of Jubilee's preoccupations had rubbed off on Clarice; she now viewed her sister's photo and her sister's name with unease. She unlocked the door. Jubilee rushed to her bureau and began to go through her drawers.

"What are you looking for?"

"My passport! They've taken my passport! He said he would put it back but he didn't."

"Who said that?

"He never tells me his name. You know who I mean." She lowered her voice, her hands still stuffed in shirts and sweaters in the second drawer. "That man with the mustache. The one who's always trying to take me away somewhere. That's why I was in detention. What's going to happen to them?" Her voice was hushed with fear. "They took some of them away. No one said a word. What could we do? They don't tell us a thing!"

Clarice had gone to the support meetings; she was always being told not to deny her sister's reality. But how was that possible? And which version of what was happening did that apply to, anyway? What Jubilee imagined was happening, changing from day to day or what was truly happening, which was a steady change from day to day. A sudden wash of weariness made her want to leave, but she took a breath and said, "You're safe now, Jubilee. I'll make sure it never happens again."

Jubilee turned sharp eyes on her. She seemed to penetrate through that lie for an instant, hearing its insincerity, its impossibility. Then she yielded to it, her eyes growing wet. "I knew I could count on you," she said.

❅ ❅ ❅

WHO WAS THIS MAN Jubilee kept seeing, who watched her from port windows, who took away her fellow residents, who drove planes and crashed trains? Who was he? Why was he the future Jubilee had settled on, the guide to her rings of hell? Was he simply an organizing principle of some kind, a thought that the incoherence in her life was made coherent by having one particular enemy?

Why that particular enemy, though?

It would be wonderful, Clarice thought, to have a person, a concrete person, to blame: to have someone to curse and batter, to let go of the resignation that she knew was the only response that made sense. Made sense—it was nonsense of course; how did the observation of madness make sense?

But the next time she came, Jubilee reported that the man with a mustache had pointed at her, and had frozen her heart for a full minute. But then he'd let her go, only to appear again in a doorway, then down the hall; one day he appeared two tables over in the dining room. He was the conductor on a runaway train; the doctor in a hospital of screams; he was the chef who poisoned the food of the woman who died two doors down.

It was he who had twisted her head so that she never completely understood where she was or what was happening.

❉ ❉ ❉

"GRANNY KNOWS WHO HE is," Jubilee said as soon as Clarice entered the bedroom. She was sitting up against the mirror again. Granny nodded back at her from the mirror, dressed (of course) exactly the way Jubilee was dressed. "Tell her who it is," Jubilee said with excitement. She motioned for Clarice to sit next to her.

Clarice hesitated; she would be facing the mirror then. That might break the illusion. Was that a good or a bad thing? She sat down.

And it didn't disrupt Jubilee at all, because Jubilee spoke to the mirror. She addressed her own image as Granny, and when she wanted to speak to Clarice, she looked at the mirror-Clarice. When Granny spoke, Jubilee moved her lips, whispering the words. Maybe that was a mirror, too—some mirror of thoughts.

"He's my neighbor. Gerry Darr. You know the white house with the blue trim across the street and down? He had a wife and then the wife disappeared. People whispered, they said she'd gone to the hospital and died there, but when it came down to it, who actually saw the ambulance?"

✳ ✳ ✳

THE NEXT TIME THE aides told her that Jubilee was in bed with a bad cold.

"Where are they taking me," Jubilee asked in a thick voice. She sat up. Her body leaned towards Clarice.

"Taking you?" Clarice looked around, trying to establish a clue to her sister's fantasy.

"This ambulance—where is it going? And how did you get here so fast? They just got me, just a minute ago. Did you hear me crying?"

Clarice took a breath. "I did. I heard you crying. As soon as I heard, I came right to you. You can always be sure of that—I'll hear you." Was that too much? Would anyone believe that?

"I knew it," Jubilee breathed. "I'm dying, right? That's why they're taking me away. I know, because *he's* driving. *He* came for me. This is the end of it for me." She broke into sobs; her misery took over everything. "I thought there was more," she cried. "I thought I could figure it out and get away."

Clarice took her hand. Her sister's fingers gripped her; the tendons in her hand stood out; she had a great deal of strength, at least in her body.

"It's not true," Clarice hissed. She was struggling not to cry as well— how lost her sister was. Wasn't it bad enough that she had no idea of reality; did she have to be this miserable as well? Did all of her days have to be spent in fear and anguish? Why was this allowed? She couldn't bear it; how could her sister bear it, adrift in a world that tormented her. What was she to do? How could she give her some peace?

She reached for a new story. "I told the police and they're running after him right now, Jubilee, maybe you can hear the shouts out in the street?" She lifted her head up and tilted it.

Jubilee's tears stopped abruptly and she raised her eyes to the window and began to listen as well. "Yes," she said in surprise. "Yes, I can hear it."

"They'll catch him, and he'll never hurt you again."

Her sister's body relaxed. "You're so good to me," she said. She whispered her thanks, over and over again, and it left Clarice feeling oddly imposed upon. Why did she have to find a way to get her sister out of the horror she was in? What would happen on the day when she began to fail? It wasn't fair, it wasn't right, any of it. Her sister was in good health, riotously good health, the doctor said—so there would be decades ahead of her, decades of obsessions and delusions, of shadowy figures and wailing about her fate. None of which Clarice could solve; all of which Clarice could see.

It wasn't fair to Jubilee; it wasn't fair to Clarice. Her head was stuffed tight with reluctance; she didn't want to continue; she didn't want to think of years and years of this; of her sister, trapped and going deeper into her world of horror; she didn't want that. And yet there it was always ahead of her, always including her.

✻ ✻ ✻

Two days later, she took the subway to the ferry terminal as usual, already dreading Jubilee, the wearying problem of Jubilee. She moved mechanically to the great windowed main room on the water, where people stood resolutely, waiting for the ferry to come in. They seemed to have assigned places; they seemed to have been there perpetually, but there was also about them a kind of organized expectation, a vigilance that struck Clarice, for the first time, as ominous.

One of them seemed to be watching her—and, with a slight slurp of horror at her heart, she saw it was a man with a mustache. For a single, shattering moment she met her sister's world—she felt the press of it— and it was horrible; it was thrilling.

With a strange and intentional twist, it all shifted.

Abruptly, she shouted, "There he is!" and deliberately knocked into a man holding a cup of coffee, knocked him into the crowd, where he stumbled against two other people, creating a stir. "That's him!" she cried. "The guy in the mustache!"

And miraculously, there *was* a man in a mustache where she was pointing, though not the same one; this one was an old man and his face went aghast as people turned towards him. The other man with a mustache had moved away.

Clarice felt the crowd shift and stir. "There he is again," she shouted, waving off into the air. "Somebody stop him—stop him before it's too late!" The crowd murmured but there was nothing specific enough to go on; people shifted back and forth, craning their necks, trying to see what was happening. Clarice felt them, felt the crowd, felt their uncertainty, their desire to be certain, to act. She made her way through them, stumbling forcefully, falling into people. She cursed them for pushing her. She cried out, "Ouch!" as loud as she could; she yelled that someone had picked her pocket. She whipped her head back and forth, her voice spilling out of her in tongues—or what she imagined was tongues, and they wouldn't know either, she thought triumphantly. For the purpose of the crowd was to find out which emotion would win: fear, anger, retribution, sorrow—all of it surged through the crowd, wanting to find a face to land on, a set of footsteps to stand in. That was what her sister knew: it was all there, waiting.

She began to spin around, her arms jammed out, and people were getting out of her way. She caught, out of the corner of her eye, the way they changed their direction, but kept their gaze on her. Of course they would; she was shouting: massive, inspirational shouts! The great doors to the ferry were opening, and she was caught a little bit on the tide of the people moving towards it—and she imagined for a moment that it was the ship Jubilee had told her about, the one caught in the massive waves, so she cried out, "There's a tidal wave coming!" and some people stopped to look out to the bay, she was sure of it. Someone closer tsk'd and called her a nutcase. People swept by her and into the ferry and she spun around to get away from them and it, letting her arms flail. There was a tidal wave coming, after all.

It felt so good to be the crazy one! She let her head fall back, let her chin scrape the high ceiling of the terminal. The crowd was pouring away from her now, the ferry swallowing bodies, heads, faces, eyes telescoping away from her. She was an avoidance ring! They looked askance at her, at her reality, much as she looked at her sister, or the way she felt she had been looking at her sister. It was a transference; for a moment she lived in the casual reality of her sister's world, giving presence to her fears, combining memory and imagination and dream. She could make anything happen.

She ran outside before someone alerted the police, before they could grab her and haul her away (as they had hauled Jubilee, she murmured; as they had hauled Jubilee).

She walked away from the terminal till her heart rate eased and her thoughts slowed down to normal thoughts.

Life, after all, was arbitrary in its gifts; it gave out sanity; it took it away. Life took the long view, the optimistic view that in the end it was all a matter of a story or a memory; that whatever Jubilee believed was indeed good enough for Jubilee.

And there was a part of her that was attracted to Jubilee's stories; she realized that suddenly, and it disturbed her.

After a few minutes, she turned back to the terminal; she was on her way to her sister, after all. But the minute she entered the great expanse of the widowed room, she froze.

It was all well and good to play at being mad; it was a form of love, to try to see how Jubilee saw it. Maybe.

But who "played at madness"? Would she play at it again? She stepped to the side of the entrance way and viewed the room—its great windows, its stark benches, the flow of people, the groups of kids out on a lark, the view through all those windows to the wide waters.

Who plays at madness? she asked herself again.

And though she longed to see Jubilee—and, she now realized, it was principally to gauge how far away she was from *being* Jubilee—though she regretted her own insulting behavior, there was a reservoir of madness all about the room; a reservoir of madness waiting on the ferry itself, with its portholes and its railing and its endless obliging waters.

She wouldn't see Jubilee today. She might not see her tomorrow. She had sinned—that was a word she hadn't used since childhood—she had sinned against Jubilee.

Clarice turned back, taking her game with her, her terrible game.

## 11

# BRIGHT BRIGHT BEDLAM

THE RESIDENTS HERE COME in two varieties: the cursers and the zombies. All of them trying to escape, one way or the other. We go chasing them down the hall when the alarms go off; we slam the doors in the dayroom and start the count, half of us minding the ones we've got and the other half checking down the halls and in their rooms, counting heads, Yvonne shouting out, "Get those numbers, now," because she likes numbers games and it's a little fun that way (though we're not supposed to think that). We find Connie, Edith, Vinny, Kevin, check the bathrooms too though a lot of them are in diapers, big baggy things that spill with adult urine and all, and of course we find the door with the alarm ringing and look out *it*, too; but not once have I ever seen the back of anyone running. Then we key in the code and the alarm stops.

Little jailbreaks. Exciting, I think. For all of us. Because we get bored, we feel pent up sometimes, though we go home when our shift is over— but every day it's back here, pulling Vinny by the hand, dealing with the endless fussing. And the cursing, which surprises everyone. Edith, small and neat and gray, sitting politely, suddenly shouting "Shit fucking piss artist, what the fuck did you say to me? You say that again and I'll crush your toes in the cement mixer you'll see what you did." Always a cement mixer, though it can be other parts of the body.

My husband, Franco, came twice hoping to catch her at it, but she was quiet both times. He's curious about this place, thinks I get too attached. But I tell him it's just the way it is when you're tending to people. You get fond of them.

Connie sits with a babydoll most of the time, cradling it, makes a good scene, the tours for the relatives like it very much as long as she doesn't get whatever it is in her head and start smacking that baby. She won't allow men near her, raises the roof then with the fucks and the shits; there's a story there. But you can't exactly go up to the son or daughter or niece or whatever and ask, Was that woman raped? Most likely, in my experience, they wouldn't even know.

Vinny, who goes up to people too close, and talks to them softy in syllables only (he has no words left), takes one of the photos Anita likes to look at and walks around with it. I take it back and put it in front of Anita. A wedding picture, not Anita's though. Vinny takes things from one place and puts them down somewhere else.

Ruby yells out, "Never mind! Electrician set off the alarm!" There's a key code you have to put in before you go out the door to keep it from ringing, otherwise you put the keycode in backwards on the outside to cancel it. The electrician should have looked that up; but they never do. But everyone's safe and Ruby, she gives a great big whoop—that's our Ruby, big and bold and brassy, always trying to kick things off. She organizes parades sometimes, just when we've all had it up to here, tells the aides to get hats and bright clothes from the residents' rooms, and then we all start lining them up and walk up and down the corridors, having a parade. We call down for Cheryl, the hairdresser, to come up, wearing one of those gowns so you don't get hair on them, and there's of course the sweeper, pushing her cart, and we turn up all the radios to different stations and for a while there's excitement like you wouldn't believe, even the wanderers fall in line, the ones who can't sit still and go from window to door, mumbling. Then shoosh! It's all over and it's time for cookies and tea. Settle them in, give them something to drink, then haul them off to the toilets one by one.

Leila's the newest aide, she sometimes seems too embarrassed to do anything easily, and she once walked towards a visitor sitting with her mother, ready to haul that visitor off to the toilet, when she caught herself just as she went to grasp her arm. She couldn't stop saying how sorry she was, but the woman didn't take it amiss, even laughed at first; if Leila had just apologized once it would have been better.

"What's that spotlight on you?" Valerie asks. She's a small black woman; there are only two black residents; the other blacks are all the aides.

"No spotlight on me, honey," Yvonne says.

Valerie lifts her hand and places it in the spotlight, which is nothing, of course, the lighting is regular. "Here," she says.

Yvonne shakes her head and moves away. "I'm going to turn that spotlight off, it's bothering you," she says and goes over the light switches on the wall and pretends to turn it off. "No more spotlight," she calls back to Valerie, who says, "It's on again," and Yvonne lets it go.

Leila watches all the other aides, learning quickly. She was afraid to touch the residents at first; I think wherever she worked before touching was frowned on, but she's got a good voice, real soothing, so I think she'll fit in eventually. She doesn't like the bathroom stuff, but who does? Bend them over when they're done, wipe their butts and get it over with; no use dwelling on it. They're babies in some ways, big fretful babies, with a strange life. Going backwards, from what I understand, losing their years, motor skills, words, inhibitions, the sense of touch is the last, we have one here in a rolling lounge chair, makes little baby hand claps, that's all she can do. Got her own aide, a cushy job that one, not always on her feet, she rolls Barbara to the sun room and grabs a snack and her cell phone. Someday I'll ask her how much she makes, how she got that job.

Because we're on our feet all day, can't put these babies in a playpen, try as we might. Some stay still, heads bowed, constantly nodding off, but the others wander around, wanting something. And as Ruby says, "I'm a big woman, you know? Hard to be on my feet all day." I love that about her, no pretense, whatever Ruby is, is fine by Ruby.

❊ ❊ ❊

CARLEENA IS POURING OUT drinks for snack time. "Any word?" I ask, not looking at her directly. Her daughter's gone missing. A fourteen-year-old with a glaring eye. Tight clothes, sharp hips. You look at her and see troubles. LaToya's been gone two months now. I have two sons; the thought of one of them out there, lost, is unbearable.

"No, nothing," Carleena says and turns away.

I take a tray and start handing out juices. They have a busy schedule, with exercise, breakfast, memory games, snacks, lunch, singing and games, snack, dinner, and movies. They can't keep track of it, of course. We take them by hand and lead them to one thing, to another thing.

"Have you seen my papers?" Edith asks; she's always looking for them, holding her hands over her fanny pack. She doesn't feel safe without it. In her old life, she never went out without her papers and her fanny pack, I guess. Her tablemate, Trudy, says sharply "You don't need those papers here."

In a little while Trudy will start crying; she's one of the ones who can't adjust, she's crazy half the time and aware of it; she keeps popping back up from wherever she goes, and she sobs.

And where does she go? What kind of place is it, and which is the right version of Trudy, of Edith, of Connie? Were the cursers always cursers, fighting it all their lives? Did the wanderers never get a chance to wander? Which is the right version—what they always were or what they are now? Have they gone now straight to their own core?

Trudy often thinks she's in prison. Her whole life long, did she secretly think she was in prison?

❖ ❖ ❖

AND HERE IT IS, Wednesday, and the Magic Man is here. We call him that because every Wednesday he sings "That Old Black Magic," without caring if anyone wants it. Sings, and pops out the same old handkerchiefs, the stuffed bunny. Once he even pulled Connie's plastic baby out of his pocket, and there was hell to pay for *that*, I can tell you. Connie went for him. We jumped then, soon as Leila cried out "Baby!" You know to act fast with Connie, if you've been here for a while. She's got a thing about that plastic baby, and a mouth that will tear your skin off.

And then, after he's gone, of course Edith starts looking for her papers.

"Forget those papers; you don't need papers," Trudy says.

"No?" Edith says uncertainly.

"What do you want those papers for anyway?"

"What time is it? Have we eaten yet?"

"I don't know what time it is!" There's a big clock on the wall opposite her; she's never noticed it. I walk by and I say, "Did someone ask the time? It's three o'clock. You've had lunch, and dinner is at five."

"Dinner is at five," Trudy shouts. "And you don't need papers. You look for them all the time, and it doesn't matter."

I walk back, and Trudy rolls her eyes. She's stuck in a wheel chair, but doesn't even know it. She doesn't want to be pushed anywhere; she wants it all to be the way it was. Whatever that means; she doesn't know. But it was different from this.

Valerie lifts her hand in the air, in a spotlight again, I suppose. She studies it intently.

We do mental exercises before dinner, and I can hear Leila going after Florence, who keeps wandering off, and I see Ruby taking Penny by the hand and sitting her down on the rows of chairs, and a few of the good ones come over naturally, interested in what's going on. Kevin feels his way along the wall to his room; he's pretty nearly blind but as long as nothing much changes he does well enough. I go and get the flash cards with the pictures on them from the cabinet, the kind my boys have grown past, they're nine and ten, and by the time I get back, I can hear it.

"I want to go home!" Trudy cries. "Help me!"

"Stop her," Carleena warns, near me at the doorway.

"Home!" Kevin bellows. His shoulders tighten.

I turn to see Margaret, silent and still, open her mouth and lift up her hand. She freezes like this sometimes when she's upset, her mouth open and pulled down, her eyes shut, her nose never wet.

Bodies start shifting around the room. "Home!" Edith cries, standing up, her hands at her fanny pack, and around the room criers and zombies alike stir, their eyes bugging, their hearts thumping.

"*Let me go home,*" Ruby begins to sing. "*Let me go home—I feel so broke up, I want to go home.*"

She sways her hips. I run over to her, grabbing Kevin on the way. I put my one hand on his shoulder, crying out, "Kevin, sing!" And begin to dance and sing.

Kevin was a singer; he hears music when he hears nothing else. He joins in and one by one the mood changes and some sing and some nod.

Ruby doesn't stop. She begins some reggae—none of the residents know it, and I don't either, but she shakes her massive hips and shimmies. "It's breaking out of me!" she calls, her head and eyes tipping to the left and then the right. "Lord, Lord, it's getting out of me!"

And Carleena runs over, her teeth stretched bright, and shrugs into a shimmy next to Ruby, singing along.

"If you ain't laughing here each and every day, you've lost your way," Ruby shouts out, wagging her butt, grabbing Penny, who stumbles gamely.

One or two go away back to their tables or over to the window, and Kevin demands to know when they'll be serving dinner, and the day moves back into place and we go back to songs about home.

Carleena has her arms raised, though, held up to the roof, her eyes raised, too, though tears run down. She keeps singing, lower and lower, twisting her hips, her feet moving a tight circle. I go next to her and raise my hands, too, and sway around with her. She can have the words, because I think the words might matter to her. All the business of home, you know, wondering if her daughter was dead or dying or wishing with her last breath to go home. Well, home is the place where you know everyone's safe, and when they're not home with you it means it could be bad. Carleena is afraid. I raise my hand and dance with her.

❅ ❅ ❅

THE NEXT DAY IS a bad day, they come without warning and no justification that I can see. Even Ruby has a grim look. She's eating coffee ice cream, and that never goes well, she'll be taking pills all day. That means she probably had a fight with Malcolm, the two of them too strong-minded to have a peaceful life. So it'll be bad for a day or so, and then it will all pick up again when she comes in with cookies or donuts, a shine on her face. The two of them will never die of boredom. But she's on afternoons, and the gloom was already there in the morning.

The exercise lady comes, so we move the chairs in two lines again and get them to sit. Edith gets up and we sit her down. Leila sits next to her, holding her hand, Kevin wanders around, feeling chairs where there shouldn't be chairs. Yvonne shouts, "Kevin! Kevin! Over here, my man!" and Kevin goes to her, complaining. He can't hear or see enough for exercises, so Yvonne takes him to his room. He listens to music there, and the surprise to me is that it isn't all that loud. He can hear music; he can't hear us.

We leave Connie with her baby. Connie usually won't join in. But she's in the main room, sitting in a room with people, and for Connie, that's interaction.

I wonder about the exercise lady—what job did she fail at to get this? Did she actually go to school to sit people in chairs and get them to raise their arms?

We all of us do the exercises—chair exercises—touch your hand to your shoulders, touch your hand to your knees. We plaster a smile, we touch our shoulder, we eyeball each other and wink, pull Vinny back in his chair, grab Edith's hand just as she's about to rise—it's like we're a chain of eyes saying, "Yes, I know. Yes, I know." What do we know? We're the guard, the guardians, we're the spirit of the place, these wrinkled children are *our* children, their sorrows now no deeper than a child's sorrow, here and gone. We keep them clean and safe, we keep them here, where nothing will harm them.

Then Kevin comes out of his room and starts bellowing that someone stole his shoes and he can't hear us shouting that he's *wearing* his shoes and he can't see us pointing to his feet to *show* him, because he's mostly deaf and blind and doesn't know it. Leila jumps up and takes him by the arm and sits him down and takes his hand and puts it on his feet so he can feel his shoes and he shouts, "What are you doing, woman?" as the exercise lady says, "Twist gently at the waist."

Vinny wanders by and quietly takes one of the exercise lady's spare music tapes. Ruby drapes her arm around his shoulder and walks him back, putting the tape back in its place. Valerie says, "Ruby, you've got a spotlight on your nose."

And I love it all at times like this. I love puppies, and toddlers, their determination to amble off and do what they don't-know-what, their unhidden neediness at times. I love everyone here, all together like this, and I deeply love Ruby and Carleena, something Franco gets grumpy about or pretends to. I come home with stories about Ruby eating ice cream and crying, "Lord, Lord, I'm going to pay for this!" and Carleena cradling Trudy in her arms as Trudy sobs that she wants to go home.

There is goodness here.

Franco grumbles that I sometimes don't know where my proper home is, but I know his heart and it's all right.

Connie starts hitting her plastic baby all of a sudden, a bad thing. I see Carleena's eyes shift and focus on that, and a big frown pulls her mouth down. Her daughter was pregnant. We all murmured when she told us that, and we all—all—thought: of course.

But now that LaToya's gone, baby belly and all, Carleena notices that doll more; we all do. Leila rushes over to Connie and calms her down. "That baby's always crying, isn't it? That's a baby for you, never any appreciation, maybe it's got gas." And so Connie starts to burp it, a good move on Leila's part, she's really getting the hang of it. Carleena stares for a while longer, then turns away. Her neck looks locked to me.

And then all the exercises end and Yvonne nudges me and says, "What's that?" There's a policeman in the doorway, but Yvonne's chin is nudging towards Carleena.

She's frozen in her tracks, holding on to Edith, a bathroom call or something, and Edith takes her hand away and walks off. Carleena's face is all eyes and mouth directed at that cop.

I think something has happened to LaToya, and Carleena thinks so too.

But the cop starts singing! Carleena's face breaks apart, she looks like she has lost her place in the world.

The singing cop goes to Vinny and takes his hand, and walks around the room and up and down the hallways, nodding at people. Vinny follows along, his lips moving.

Sharon, the administrator, must have let him in 'cause I see her here watching. "It's Vinny's birthday," Sharon says. "He used to be a police officer. That's his nephew." She looks around. "Seems to be going well."

She's looking at the residents, of course. She's not looking at Carleena, who anyway has caught her breath and is drinking a cup of water, one arm steadying herself against the counter.

"You see that?" Ruby says a little later.

"Well, LaToya's still missing. Maybe she thought it was bad news."

"Nuh," Ruby says. "She thought it was *worse* bad news. She didn't cry out. I've been thinking she knows something, the way she's keeping quiet. You ask her, 'Anything new about LaToya?' And she just says no. If you were worried to distraction, you'd be talking, right?"

"She did at first," I agree. "Nonstop."

"She knows something. She knows where LaToya is, and it ain't good."

❋ ❋ ❋

SOME PEOPLE NEVER GET visitors, but we lie and say they do. We say, "Valerie, what a handsome son you have, and I could see how much he loves you!" Valerie's son came once exactly. We saw him, we keep track.

We listen for what they say, we hover everywhere, listening. Sometimes Ruby, after she's made up with Malcolm, will come with her box of donuts and say, "Edith, your daughter sent these. Look, there's a note." And it's a note that Ruby wrote, of course, but day by day we tell the ones who never get visitors that they *just* had visitors, and discuss those visitors all to hell—"Hey, Yvonne, Penny thinks her sister was wearing the pink sweater, but it was blue, wasn't it?"—we talk them into being real. We can do that, we can give them a moment of being remembered, keep them thinking their loved ones are faithful; we can do that.

❄ ❄ ❄

CONNIE LEAVES THAT PLASTIC baby of hers, every so often. She'll sit with the others at activities, smiling in a superior way. If Kevin or Vinny gets too close she'll start with "Go away, you fucking shit bastard" and Kevin will give it right back at her, but Vinny murmurs his nonsense syllables in a pleading voice, stopping right in front of her. Then Yvonne or Leila takes his hand and leads him away.

He picks up things and puts them down somewhere else; he never takes anything to his room. He's always moving; we're used to it. We can judge how long it will take him to reach the doorway, get out of sight in the hallway; it comes natural after a while, so we only keep a bit of an eye out for him; he's harmless; that's how we miss seeing what he does.

It's the last activity before dinner, so they're all in the small common room, next to the dining room, when I hear a scream that stabs my heart. Carleena is screaming, then wailing, and I hear Ruby yelling out, "What is it? What is it?"

I tell Leila to stay with them, and she nods and calls for Yvonne, and I run to the kitchenette, where Carleena is bent over, sobbing, and Ruby has her hand on Carleena's shoulder, moving her sort of, pushing Carleena backwards. I look around, fast, and see nothing alarming.

Carleena heaves herself upright, then folds over again. Ruby has her by the forearms, now, pushing her backwards. It's like a slow dance. Behind Ruby, in the corner, is the garbage can, and I sidle over slowly, get behind Ruby, blocking the view, and look in.

It's Connie's plastic baby, and it comes together, all at once: a pregnant daughter, a baby in the garbage, and cops.

Carleena is heaving her sorrows up, right there in front of us. Vinny is coming towards her, murmuring his syllables, his hands gesturing, and Yvonne comes and takes him. No doubt he moved that doll, the way he moves things, just from one place to another, no special reason, but this time he's caused chaos. I yank the doll up quiet as I can and put it behind me, going to a bathroom to rinse it off fast and get it back before Connie looks for it and *that* screaming adds to the woe.

I dry it and put it back.

I hear Ruby's soothing voice, and Carleena's voice rising and rising, I don't catch the words. Then there's silence, and I see Ruby coming for me, and all at once the alarms go off and there's no choice, we have to follow instructions, closing the ones in the common room, leaving Yvonne and Leila to take count there, then Ruby yells, "Maybe that's Carleena," but of course Carleena knows the combination, and Ruby goes toward the front door and I go to the back exit.

I run and fling it open, not bothering with the key code to stop the alarm because I see Carleena at the far end of the hall, at the elevators, and I yell over my shoulder, "Ruby! She's getting away!" but just a glance backwards shows me that Edith is following me, her hands on her fanny pack and a frightened look on her face and I feel I can't just leave like that, slamming the door in Edith's face. Even though I want to, I really do, and for a split second I consider it because my heart is breaking for Carleena, and it's Carleena who needs help now, but Edith is my responsibility; Carleena will come back.

I put in the code and close the door and take Edith's hand and we go back to the common room.

Yvonne looks at Edith. "Everyone's here," she says, tapping the sheet with the residents' names on it.

"Carleena's not here," I say. "Carleena is missing." They don't answer me at first, because it's true and because Carleena isn't part of the count.

"Carleena just wanted to go home," Ruby says, but it's the wrong thing to say because I can see Trudy sitting up and her mouth is falling open and I know what's coming next. Ruby doesn't see it, but I do and I can't stand the idea of it, of the fuss she'll make, without Carleena here to lift her arms up. I rush over to Trudy and I kneel beside her and I say, "This is home. You are home. This is home," over and over until Ruby puts her hand firm on my shoulder and Trudy looks away.

# 12

## 242

HER MOTHER WAS IN the crazy ward. Visitors had to check their coats, their cellphones, their bags, their hoodies if they wore a hoodie, before they could go in. And after they let the visitors through the locked doors, they couldn't go to the patients' rooms. Instead, the patients came to the visiting room; some were pushed in a geriatric chair, a kind of rolling lounge chair, to the visiting room, which was very small. The overflow went to the hallway.

Alice saw her mother sitting hunched over to the side, in the hallway. in her geri-chair. Her mother had been moved to the psychiatric ward because of her behavior problems; the nursing home had sent her to the hospital to have her tested for a physical cause; the hospital had moved her to this floor. Alice had put her head on the table when the hospital had called. All this time her mother thought she was in prison and now, here it was!—Alice was putting her in prison.

"Mom!" she said.

Her mother's face lit up. "You're amazing," her mother said.

Alice bent over and kissed her. "Why am I amazing?"

"You always find me."

"I'll always find you," Alice answered. She smiled broadly, trying to cover how bad she felt. She felt cheap; manipulative; selfish. She'd been saying this for weeks now: "Wherever you go, I'll find you." Her mother believed she was being moved from one prison to another. Alice had thought, at first, that this would comfort her mother, that she would think of it as she worried over her imprisonment. But was it mean, this little lie, this playing along with her mother's delusion?

"Are you afraid?" Alice asked. "I couldn't take it if you were afraid."

"I'm not afraid," her mother answered neutrally. "Why would I be afraid?"

That stopped Alice. Had she suggested fear to her mother, who could run with her delusions? Had she planted something else now? It was terrible to feel that she could influence her, as she had with her statement about finding her.

"Not at all," Alice said firmly. "And how are you feeling?"

Her mother shrugged. "When can I go home? They won't let me out of here."

"I'll talk to them." It was a weak thing to suggest. How weak she always felt, "finding" her mother again, having no way to rescue her. She should be able to do something, but the way her mother yelled constantly now meant that the nursing homes didn't want her; she upset everyone, the other patients, the visitors. Her mother had slapped an aide. It couldn't be much of a slap, her mother couldn't even sit up without help. But her mother's fury kept surfacing. Her mother! Fury!

"Help me!" her mother began to yell. "Help me!"

"Mom, stop."

"Help me, Alice! I wanna go home! Let me out of here! Why won't you help me, Alice!"

Alice took both her mother's hands. "I'm right here, don't yell."

"Help me!" The cries were automatic.

"Why are you yelling?"

Her mother got that internal look. "I don't know," she said soberly. "Help me!"

"Mom!"

"Help me!"

"You have to stop," Alice said sternly. "You can't keep yelling. How can I help you?" She held her mother's hands tightly. Her mother twitched and held on tightly in return.

"I don't want to yell," she said. "Help me!"

"Stop!"

"Help me!"

"Stop or I'll leave."

Her mother looked at her, paused, tightened her mouth.

Good, Alice thought; that worked. Her mother's eyes moved restlessly, settling on the plaque that held the number of the vacant room she was parked next to.

"I saw a movie," Alice began, trying to find some distraction.

Her mother's mouth opened slightly, her lips moved, but she was silent.

"Two," her mother suddenly yelled.

"Stop it."

"Two-four," she yelled.

"Two-four-two," she yelled again. "Two-four, two-four-two!"

The room number on the wall. An aide brought a chair for Alice, giving a quick glance at her mother, and so she sat down, still holding her mother's hands.

"Two, two-four-two!"

"That's just a room number, it doesn't mean anything. Don't look there, look at me," she said.

"Two-four-two!" Her mother continued to yell steadily, her body rocking with the effort.

"I can't stand it," Alice said, gritting her teeth. "Tell me what you did today."

Her mother's eyes roamed back to her. "I don't know."

"Did you eat?"

"I don't know."

"Are they nice here? Are they good to you?"

"Alice," her mother said sharply. "Are you all right? Do you need money?"

"I'm fine, I have money, don't worry about me."

"I don't have any money here. I can't find my purse."

"You don't need a purse. Everything is paid for already. See? It's like a spa." She clenched her teeth. "You get meals, you get a nice place to stay, and everyone is good to you, right?" How could she tell? How could she know? "How do you feel? Do you feel all right?"

"Help me," her mother said weakly.

"Why do you do that? Why do you ask for help?"

"I don't know. Help me!"

"Mom, I miss you," Alice said weakly. "I don't know how to help you." She began to cry.

"What's wrong?" her mother asked, and her voice sounded normal. "Is something wrong? Do you go out? To that place, you know—" She took a hand out of Alice's grip and waved it. "Where they have things. Where they have things." Her free hand circled in the air.

"Movies? Work? Yes, I go out. I'm fine. It's you I'm worried about."

"Don't worry," her mother said. She had popped up again, the real mother. "I can take care of it. Are you warm enough? Do you want a cup of tea? I'm making dinner," she added thoughtfully.

"I just ate," Alice said. "It's fine. It will be spring soon, and we'll go out and take a stroll outside. You'd like that, wouldn't you?" She had a sudden inspiration. "We'll plant some flowers. You like lots of different colors, don't you? I like things to be the same shades. But I do love flowers," she added quickly.

"Help me!"

"I can't help you," Alice said wearily. "Unless you tell me what to do. What should I do?"

"Oh, Alice," her mother said sharply, "figure it out for yourself."

Alice stiffened. "No," she said angrily. "You figure it out. Figure out what you want. And I'll get it. I'll find it. Tell me what you want."

"I want to go home," her mother cried. "Why won't you help me?"

She had to change the way this visit was going; they kept getting worse and worse. If only she could distract her mother, change the topic, change the mood. "I brought the paper," she said, pulling out the section she'd smuggled in her purse—for all she knew, news was forbidden here. "Do you want to know what's happening? There's been a tidal wave, an earthquake, some politician in the news."

"I don't care," her mother shouted. "Why won't you leave me alone? Why are you always bothering me? Look what you've done!" She gestured with her hand, to the hallway, to the number on the wall, which caught her eye again. "You! Two! Two-four-two!"

Alice asked to see a nurse, who came as Alice sat huddled next to her mother, who was still yelling the room number.

"She's due for a pill in an hour," the nurse said. "I'll see if we can give it to her sooner."

"Does she yell all the time?" Alice asked. "Or just when I'm here?"

The nurse shrugged. "This isn't my usual ward," she said. "So I don't know." She walked off, in search of the doctor.

"Does anyone know?" Alice asked the aide, who stood near her. The aide said, "She just got here, you see. Sometimes they're quiet while they're trying to figure it out. I heard her yell a little, yes."

It filled her head suddenly, her mother falling quiet as she looked around, trying to calculate where she was, trying to make some kind of explanation for it. Keeping low as her brain sorted through things, taking a piece of this and that and stitching it together. Constantly coming to the same conclusion: I have been taken away, I am in prison, I am locked up, I am alone.

Alice grabbed her mother's hands again, holding them firmly. For one second, she thought to herself, willing her thoughts to reach across the divide and pierce her mother's brain, for one second you will realize there is someone with you. Right here, right now: I am with you.

# 13

## THE YEAR OF HIS FATHER

BOYD CAME FOR AN hour almost every day. He nodded to familiar faces in the hallway, sat down next to his father's bedside, shifted into position, his hands clasped and hanging between his knees, his eyes roaming back and forth from his father's face to the walls, the floors, the tops of cabinets, to the various signs identifying the nurse and floor doctor, the phone number for the patient advocate. He didn't really read them; his eyes just drifted.

His father used to be a huge man, a man who had eaten and drunk steadily. Though he had always argued for moderation, dammit, he'd moved less after hurting his back, and fell to eating. He'd had a belly that lifted the sheets up for a foot or so, originally. When he'd still been able to eat. For a while Boyd tried to imagine the old stomach there, like a phantom limb, a ghost belly. He kept thinking it was like someone had come in and sliced it right off, all of it gone. Taken somewhere.

Up until the incident, his father had been a serious man. Even an angry man. He thought most people were stupid and the proof was all around. He was physical; his hands had round, flat fingertips, hard palms with hard bits of skin always lifting off; he had scars on his knuckles and along the top of his hands. He worked in factories, doing something with metal. Boyd had never been interested in what his father did.

At the nursing home, Boyd sat next to his father, watching and waiting. There was no hope left; it was merely a question of wondering when his father would die, of being weirdly balanced between hoping it would come soon and being ashamed of that. He believed you should be grateful for what you had—probably his father's basic instructions. Don't be a complainer. Do what has to be done. Face it squarely. And every minute his father was alive should be counted as a blessing; theoretically.

Though if his father were in this room now, alive as he used to be, it was hard to figure what he'd say about it. He was coldly practical. He had decided, for instance, when the dog needed to be put down—even though the dog was still eating and moving around. His father had studied Teddy for a week, seeing things Boyd hadn't seen, and then the dog was gone.

If he were here right now, he might be capable of striding over to that figure in the bed and putting a plastic bag over its head. And Boyd would admire that, respect that, approve that—everything in fact except be capable of doing that.

He and his father hadn't gotten along. His father had never approved of him—he was too soft, too "artistic"—though Boyd had never been interested in any kind of art. It was true that he was a troublemaker—breaking things, skipping school, getting drunk as often as he could from the time he was ten—but not for any higher calling. He just didn't like being told what to do. That was pretty much the one rule he had, and it ran smack up against his father's rule, which was that everyone had to do what he said. His father had oozed disapproval like an oil on his skin. In turn, Boyd had staked his own territory by the time he was 15. He stayed out at night and came home drunk. One time, puking, his father had kicked him. Fine.

Twice, his father locked him out.

As if that was hard to handle! Boyd could climb up to the second floor and raise his own window, and when he came home once and found the window locked, he had no hesitation in breaking the glass.

They battled each other furiously. By 16, Boyd had taken his father's car a dozen times, once crushing the front right bumper. His father punched him for that one. Boyd was almost big enough to punch him back. He stole things from the local stores and mostly got away with it, but then he got caught. His father was called. His father said he was too busy to bail him out until the next day.

And in fact, Boyd enjoyed his jail visit. He could live off the notoriety for years, he figured. Girls instantly wavered around him, watching him, bug-eyed. The jocks paid him some respect.

"I was just checking it out," he said, in front of the girls. "Seeing how it fits."

He dropped out of school soon after that. He stayed out late with his friends, and sometimes he didn't come home at all. He found a part-time job bagging groceries.

"You're better than that," his father said. "Or maybe you're not. What do you think—is that all you're good for?"

Boyd was ready for it; he had practiced his grin. He got it right: just a grin, no shame, no embarrassment. "Of course not. They said I could be a cashier someday."

His father was disgusted and walked away. That was a little disappointing.

By then, his father took the battery out of his car at night and hid his wallet and even locked up the refrigerator—no extra food for his oaf of a son!—and Boyd found a way around everything. He bought weed with his meager earnings from the grocery, then began to sell it, small stuff, but he got caught. He was still 16, and the judge was lenient.

He learned that his father was the one who had alerted the cops.

That had been shocking. A friend of a friend was the son of the cop who busted him, and that's how he heard. Even then, he couldn't believe it.

He showed up for dinner one night, surprising both his parents. He took out $100 and placed it next to his father's fork. "I hear you gave me up to the cops. Is it true?"

His father chewed slowly.

His mother slammed her glass on the table and glared at her husband. "Well, Riley? Did you turn him in?"

"For his own good," his father said, not looking either of them in the eye. "What's the money for?"

"For this," Boyd said, and grabbed a plate of food and slammed it on his father's head. It felt good. It felt like he'd violated every taboo in the world. He heard his mother yelling for him to stop, but he didn't want to stop. His father got up, staggered a little, then lifted his fist and aimed it at Boyd, who side-stepped it just enough to have it land on his shoulder rather than his face.

"Good God, the two of you," his mother said bitterly, and she stepped over to the sink and ran some water into a pot.

His father was off-balance and Boyd picked up a platter and brained him with it.

There was a pause and then his mother threw the water on them both. Boyd shook it off, but his father continued to stagger backwards, his arm reaching out for a chair. He lowered himself in it, his eyes downcast. Blood began to trickle from his head.

"I'm calling the ambulance," his mother said. She began dialing, her back turned towards the table. Her voice had cracked; his proud mother, Boyd realized, was upset. "Boyd, I think you'd better get your things together and stay somewhere else for a while."

Boyd's father said nothing; he sat there, his head lowered, as blood dripped off him onto the floor. Boyd got a rag and dropped it at his father's feet. Then he went to his room and grabbed a bag of clothes.

He walked down the street to the corner, where he heard the ambulance before he saw it. He sat down on some front steps, looking like he belonged, and called a friend to come pick him up. The ambulance went away again before his friend arrived.

❊ ❊ ❊

SITTING BESIDE HIS FATHER, he wondered, again, how much longer he would have to come here, and then he thought with a small shiver that he would miss it when it stopped. Strangely, yes, there was something calming about sitting there, all activities ceased, a kind of static existence, where he could think or not think. He favored not thinking.

That never lasted long. He went through his memories, ticking them over, most of the time, like an old nun with her beads.

He hadn't spoken to his father for almost ten years when his mother called to say she was dying and his father needed him. "What about you?" he'd asked, almost crying, "don't you need me?"

"I need this," she told him. "I can't do this without the two of you reconciled. And I can't leave him alone. You don't know that about him, but I do. You've cut into his heart."

"I have a heart, too," he said gruffly. "I wouldn't turn a son of mine in to the cops."

"He did it for your own good."

"And see how well that turned out."

But he came back home, to his gaunt mother, to his silent, angry father.

He found out that the ambulance had called the police for a domestic dispute when they found his father in the kitchen. His mother had been taken in for questioning, then released as his father insisted he'd just fallen down. He was stitched up and discharged from the hospital.

"I'm sorry, mom," Boyd said. "I didn't know."

"There's a lot you don't know," his father said. He had a hard time keeping the anger out of his voice. Boyd shut his own mouth for a change. He was older; he paid more attention to why people said what they did. Plus, he'd had an ex-girlfriend who told him she was pregnant with someone else's baby and left town. He didn't know what to believe on that one. Had she been lying about whose baby it was? Did he have a kid out there somewhere? He couldn't find her, not even by searching on the internet. He thought she'd changed her name. He thought he'd never know.

He'd married, eventually. A woman a little older than he was. She was kind and steady but she couldn't have any kids. It was strange to think he was technically the end of the line for his family. Maybe that was good. He couldn't imagine having a kid like he'd been.

❊ ❊ ❊

HE AND HIS FATHER formed a truce, and over the years they slipped into a grudging kind of relationship. No talking about old wounds, that kind of thing. About five years ago, he'd taken his father out—it was Father's Day perhaps?—a dull dinner somewhere, with the requisite two Manhattans, his father's idea of a celebration. They had been talking about—what? A news item? They often resorted to news items. Some scandal. They steered carefully away from any real conversation. Boyd was nearing 40; his father nearing 70.

No, they'd been talking about TV shows, something safe, and Boyd had just said something about getting a DVR when his father made a strange sound.

Boyd looked up and his father started to laugh.

His father never laughed like that, loud and open mouthed, merry faced.

"Dad?" he'd asked tentatively. They hadn't been discussing anything funny. His eyes darted around; maybe he'd missed something?

His father roared.

"Dad?"

"I do think," his father said, gasping in hilarity, "I do think something's happened. I think I've had a stroke!" Tears ran down his face, from laughing so hard.

Boyd had been stunned for a minute at least, watching his father's face, listening to him roar "har har har har har!" and trying to figure it out. A stroke? How could this be a stroke? He sat until he could no longer stand it, then he went to the maitre d' and asked someone to call 911. He hadn't had a cell phone at that point, that's how long ago it was. Five years, minimum.

They waited for the ambulance, and his father got silent. Maybe they were both remembering the last time an ambulance had come for him, after Boyd had cracked his head.

Boyd asked, "How do you feel, dad?"

His father answered, "I don't feel right, Boyd."

Then, as soon as the paramedics arrived, he began again.

Laughed all the way to the E.R. It was terrifying. Boyd called his wife, Pat, who rushed to join him. She was the one who held her father's hand when he wasn't being hauled off for a scan of this and a scan of that. Little clutches of doctors came by—two of them, three of them, writing down notes, asking the same questions other doctors had already asked. It took the whole night.

So. Pseudobulbar Affect. From a stroke or a disease or a tumor. Well known, in the right circles. People, it seemed, were laughing all over the U.S. when they weren't crying. Because they'd had an event. A brain event. He and Pat listened soberly; his father laughed, again.

It was a year or so before the additional diagnosis—Alzheimer's too; not just this PSA thing. By then, his father had gone from the steady saturnine man that Boyd knew to a man given over to moments of laughter and even, occasionally, outbursts of tears. He would sometimes comment on himself: "Oh boy, here it goes! Seized by the humors!" This strange attempt to make a joke of it—a perplexing attempt to be a new kind of person, perhaps; a blend of the old and the new—annoyed Boyd. He could feel his own face grow red as his father's outbursts got no better; even in the beginning, it seemed possible that his father was doing it, doing it deliberately, testing him or punishing him. But it didn't stop, and Boyd tried to adjust.

He dutifully suggested movies or dinners, for birthdays and such, always hoping that his father would refuse. Indeed, once his father's eyes had lifted to his (in his memory, his father always seemed to be sitting) and after a moment, he'd said, "No, let's just watch a video and you order some Chinese. Why give all our money away, hey?" That last "hey" did it, that time, whether the rhyme of it or the fact that it wasn't what he would normally say—he hugged himself with laughter.

Pat was always better with it. Pat would laugh with him. "Boyd, it's a disease," she'd say to her husband, barely containing her own impatience.

"It's just—it's not him," Boyd protested.

"It is now. He has no control. He knows it's happening. Be bigger than that; accept the fact that it's changing him. I'm sure he hates it. Don't add to it by hating him."

Of course that was the problem—he did hate this new father. He had long ago reconciled with the stiff man his father was; he didn't think he could reconcile with the laughing man his father was. It required more versatility than he had, to be honest; more than he would ever have.

He kept trying, however. He took his father to comedies when they went to the movies, so his laughter wouldn't be out of place. He took his father to family restaurants, where his father's sobs or laughs were muffled by the shrieks of kids. He and Pat took Riley with them for a weekend at a music festival—his father liked music—and Boyd watched as strangers were kind to Riley when he cried. His father was changing physically—his leg dragged, he stooped; he slurred words or lost track of what he was saying and he had a strangely ill-fitting smile on his face. Some people—those with Alzheimer's in the family—understood. Boyd could see a connection, occasionally, a recognition as someone heard him speak, heard the repetitions in his questions now, and turned to his father. Not many. One or two. Boyd didn't like to have his business known. His father, on the other hand, began to display an eagerness for a stranger's sudden hello. His mouth opened and hung open; it was unpleasant.

❧ ❧ ❧

BOYD'S WIFE, PAT, CAME in and put her hand on Riley's hand. "Hi, dad," she said. "It's Pat." She looked over at her husband. "And Boyd. It's a cool day today, a small breeze, not too much. I was looking at the garden section at the store, looking at the plants, you know? Maybe try some new vegetables this year. Why not? A few dollars for the seeds, won't kill me if they don't grow."

She turned slightly and squeezed Boyd's shoulder before pulling up another chair and sitting next to the bed. "Did you eat?" she asked her husband. It was a silly question; Boyd would eat when he got home and she would have the food ready to be warmed up. She just had a ritual; she had said once that Riley might be listening; she was speaking to Boyd but she spoke for Riley.

"What's for dinner?" Boyd answered, shrugging. It was better to play along with Pat; he spoke for his father's benefit.

"We'll pick something up on the way back. I went to the garden center; I ran a little late. Actually," she said, lowering her voice a little, "I went to volunteer at the dementia association."

He didn't answer; she knew how he felt about it. Not seriously against it, but he hated it when people took up causes because they were affected by them. And she wasn't even the man's daughter. Affected: maybe. Not related, so no danger for her. Of course he thought about it affecting him; he was the one who should go.

"I heard a story," she said, her voice going back to normal. "Still amazes me. One of the volunteers said that in one of the groups, a man whose wife had Alzheimer's met a woman whose husband had just died of it. They paired up! Can you imagine? I mean, his wife was still alive." She shook her head. "*Someone* has to do the laundry, right, Boyd?"

He looked back at her steadily. "Right indeed," he said.

"Would you do that?" she asked, raising her eyebrow.

He grinned, all of a sudden. "You think there's someone else out there who would put up with me? Tell me who, please, just so I can get an idea of the range."

She tapped his hand, a mock slap.

They murmured back and forth; a nurse came in and checked something; his father's eyes opened and he stared at nothing.

❋ ❋ ❋

A FEW YEARS BACK, Boyd had had to make a decision. His father was an independent man, who went about to meetings and council sessions after he retired; he had plenty of community contacts.

He started missing meetings, or showing up on the wrong day. His clothes became loose and dirty. When Boyd came, he shuffled off to the kitchen to get something, and came back with a hammer. Boyd had him re-tested to see how the Alzheimer's was progressing. Riley fell into the lower numbers now; he was dropping fast. Boyd got him an aide, and he locked the aide out. Boyd gave the aide the keys, and his father called the police. The aide wouldn't come back, and thus began a month-long search for an aide who would tolerate Riley—abusive now, even when laughing or crying; shouting and racially insulting.

Then assisted living. Then the calls from assisted living as his father fell down or hit someone, and three times when Riley had had another stroke and been rushed to the hospital. Boyd's heart froze when the phone rang at night, as well it should. What had his father done now? Inside his head he heard himself say he'd be glad when this was all over; it was shocking. He knew his obligations; he respected his father. He wanted his father to be safe and well.

Though safe and well were no longer possible. Well, "safe," maybe, though Riley fell often and tried to escape. But it wasn't a safety that included freedom from harm. His body was harming itself.

He often found Pat already there when he visited the assisted living place. Pat sat and chatted with Riley; Pat laughed when Riley laughed. Boyd heard them as he approached down the hallway, heard the merriment, the connection. But there was no merriment, was there? Connection—he had to admit there might be a connection; his father's shoulders looked relaxed when Boyd entered the room, the two of them conspiratorial, heads bent together. Their eyes would look up and he could tell—he wasn't making it up—his father had reached himself again.

But the years went by like a syrup. The year Riley stopped walking was also the year he started wearing diapers; the year he forgot who Boyd was turned into the year he forgot who he was; the year he stopped being able to swallow turned into the year he slept. Which was where they were now, the sleeping year. It wasn't too hard to see that next year would be death. Maybe even this year.

There were strange landmarks in Boyd's life now. For instance, he had been deeply grieved when his father had stopped holding hands, but the fact that they had even held hands was bizarre. They were not a demonstrative family: a peck on the cheek to his mother; a nod to his dad. However he came to it, he held his father's hand only after Riley was confined to bed and his eyes got a frightened, furtive look. Boyd noticed it and picked up Riley's hand and said, "Dad, it's so good to see you." And his father had grasped back eagerly, longingly. And what was abnormal at first became the norm and he liked holding his father's hand. It was not what he knew of his father, but there was something so sad in how his father wanted to hold hands—it was hard to reconcile. He had lost the man who wouldn't do it; he had gained the man who would.

His wife, who had started going to talks and meetings at various organizations when Riley was moved to the assisted living place, always had an explanation for him; she was good at feeling out her husband's emotions.

"They drop, and you adjust to the way they are—the new normal," Pat had said. "And when they drop again, you mourn again. Each time you have to say farewell, to lose another part of them. And then you get used to it, and then…"

"Yes, yes," he'd said, impatient. "They drop again. I get it."

"Do you?" she'd asked. She hadn't been annoyed; she had tilted her head to look at him. "I suppose you do. I suppose you would." She came over and gave him a little kiss on the cheek and a pat on the arm, and it was all he could do to hold himself together. That little gesture, that little acknowledgement—really, was there something wrong with him? Was he getting soft?

The day came when his father failed to hold his hand—in fact he moved it out, let it drop. It was a small thing; perhaps the next day would be different.

It wasn't. The year his father wouldn't hold his hand.

The strange thing was that sitting there with a man who couldn't speak, move or swallow, who didn't know where he was or what he was—he had never felt so close to him, never felt such an anxious affection for him. This must be what it was like to watch a newborn as it slept—looking at every muscle twitch, interpreting every moan. Interpreting the silence, now; how sad the silence was; how full.

If they'd been different people, they might have been friends now. That was his own personal joke. But when his father's personality had been stripped away; when his father had surreptitiously turned into his child— then the maneuvering between father and adult son had stopped; they had arrived at an emotional connection that had never been there before.

Three years in, the laughter stopped. His father's silent years began, when there was just a word or two, a sentence occasionally, rising up like the sight of a bird, then gone.

Occasionally, Boyd felt that his father should have tried harder to resist his decline. Did he have some weird misguided idea that it was voluntary, this disease? Occasionally, yes, that was exactly how he felt. He felt his father had left him, and even though he remembered the years of his own youth when his father's advice came at him swiftly and unwanted—finally, he missed him.

What was life like for his father as he slipped away? Did he dream? It wouldn't be so bad if his father dreamed his way to the end. Was it possible that his brain had ceased to dream? He had no idea. He would ask, but what comfort would the answer bring? What if they said no, what if his father lay there not dreaming, not thinking, emptying out drop by drop, occasionally aware (as when he opened his eyes or moaned) that something was wrong, something fundamentally wrong and he wanted so much to ask for help? What then?

Boyd now had a slightly different understanding of help. He knew he was a proud man, too; a man raised by a proud father; who looked on seeking help as weakness; who thought that all of life's ills had to be met alone, not changed, not shared. He was sorry his father had been like that; he was sorry for his father's life, he supposed.

Once, at the end of his father's laughing phase, Boyd had said, "You know, I never heard you laugh when I was a child." It was just an observation.

"I know," his father said. "I don't know why that was." His voice had regret in it. And, cruelly, something he thought about often now and regretted enormously, Boyd had answered, "Yeah, I don't know why that was, either," and his father had looked up at him with his filmy eyes, just looking. Boyd thought you could hide a room in his father's eyes, it was so hard to read them. He just wished he'd said it was all right, instead. Why hadn't he? Had he really felt he missed his father's laughter so much? It was a troubling thought to him, that he could surprise himself that way; that he didn't know himself.

He leaned over and took his father's hand and held it. His father slept on, silent. The two of them, he thought; encased in barriers in ways he hadn't expected. Had they done well enough with each other? Had they had a good life? It didn't mean anything, did it—not having laughed enough; having laughed too much? Would it have been better if his father had cried more instead of laughing? Laughter had been imposed on him. That was confounding. Laughter had been his ordeal.

He sat back, listening to himself. It wasn't the laughter that mattered, he was sure of it. The laughter had spilled out of him like a burst of blood. And like blood, it had left a stain.

He was at a loss for metaphors. His father was dying; his father had already died. He was trying to understand it all; he was giving his father's death calibrations and irony, struggling to reconcile—what?

There was nothing to reconcile. He saw that and yet he halted in front of it. It was the year of his father's dying; how could that be all there was?

# 14

# THE STRAY CURSE

THIS IS THE KIND of thing that happens all the time, though not to everyone and not everywhere.

Gina had long brown hair and brown eyes and smooth skin and a mother she didn't see everyday; she was grown and had her own world and that was the way it should be. Gina's mother had left her mother, who had left her mother, a long string of mothers being left and knowing they had done it in turn, and turn again.

But all of a sudden Gina felt a strange tug at her back. It began with an itch, then a bruise, then a feeling like there was a hook in her spine. She turned around to see what it was, and as soon as she turned the pain went away. But when she shrugged and turned again, it came back fierce and strong. She couldn't move forward; it hurt her back; she turned around and took a step then a hurried step. She was sure it was her mother pulling her home.

She ran faster and faster the closer she got, flinging the door open when she reached her mother's house.

Her mother wasn't there. She called out to her. No answer.

She ran around the back to the woods (her mother was the last house before the wilderness) and then down to the local pond where her mother liked to swim. She stood on the little dock the town had built. Her eyes traveled restlessly, and she was about to turn back when she glanced down.

There below her, deep in the water, her mother reached an arm up; it didn't break through the surface; her mother's lips were moving.

Gina dropped to her knees and reached down as far as she could. Her fingertips touched her mother's wrist; but she couldn't grab hold and pull her up. She put her ear to the water.

She could hear her mother distantly yelling, Gina! Gina! Help me! Gina, help me!

"Grab my hand!" she yelled back at her mother, but her mother couldn't.

Gina decided to jump in, but strangely enough she flattened out on the water and she couldn't reach down any further than she had before.

She felt frantic; she couldn't understand why she couldn't reach her.

"You'll never get her that way," a voice said, startling her. "She's cursed."

She turned to the man who'd spoken. "Cursed! Who would curse her? She's never hurt anyone or anything."

The man, lounging on a life guard's chair tipped against a tree trunk, straightened up and shrugged. "Well, does it matter? Do you want to find out who did it or do you want to undo it? Two different tracks entirely."

"I want to free her!" Gina cried.

"Well, okay, but you know how it is with curses. There's always a trick to getting them undone." He was a slight man with dirty hair and a dirty cap that once used to be blue.

"Can I trust you?" Gina asked impulsively.

He walked towards her. "Of course you can. I'm a *life guard*. I know all about curses; I've even given out a few in my time. Before you ask, it wasn't me. I'm older than I look and I'm much more cautious. In the past,

I've regretted a few things I've done, so I don't do them as quickly as I used to." He smiled faintly; it made Gina feel a little surer, that smile

"Then what should I do to release her?"

At that he frowned, as if he'd suddenly thought of an obstacle. "It isn't all that easy," he said. "Curses are meant to stay. Of course," he added thoughtfully, "all curses are a series of trades. There's always a little crack."

"What's the crack?" she demanded.

"Hard for me to know, I'm not active anymore." He closed his eyes dramatically and took a deep breath, then opened them again. "You need advice from someone with more connections. The school nurse comes across the young and the emerging, and they're more likely to be the ones to let a stray curse go, in case it *is* a stray curse. Yes, go to the school nurse; I think that should do it."

"But I can't leave her here," she cried.

"Of course not." He handed her a jar. When she glanced at it she saw her mother deep in the murky waters of the jar.

"Why can't I just tip it over? Why is she so small?"

"She's the same size, the water's the same size, the problem's the same size. I just changed the perspective, of course."

Gina put the jar up to her eyes. She could faintly hear her mother yelling, "Help me, Gina!"

"Go ahead," the man said, and Gina reached her fingers in through the top of the jar and found that her hand was tiny and there was the same old problem: her mother was beneath the water calling for help, and Gina couldn't reach her. She pulled her hand up.

"What can I do?"

"You have to take her with you to the school nurse; she's very wise. But I have to warn you, she'll make a hard bargain. Harder than mine, at least."

"You're bargaining something?"

"I'm making it possible to take your mother with you; without that you might lose track of her completely. Don't you think that's valuable?"

"Of course, of course," Gina said hastily.

"For that I only ask for your toes." He looked modestly away.

Gina was struck with a sudden bolt of terror. "Why would you want my toes? What a terrible thing to ask for!"

"I could have asked for a lung—surely you see how reasonable I am? I hope you won't insult me by refusing? I'd have to take my gift back." He reached for the jar, which Gina hastily hid behind her back.

"All right," she said, and closed her eyes for an instant as a quick piercing pain hit both her feet and when she opened her eyes her toes were gone—and so was the man.

She did little hops for a short distance until she learned how to walk without toes—really, it was a waddle of a sort, flat-footed of a sort—and as she got used to it she got better at it. Her feet slid around in her shoes now since the shoes were clearly too big without toes to fill them. She stopped and tore her sleeves off, and wadded them into the toes of her shoes. There was no blood.

The school nurse was sitting at her desk, filling in forms. She looked up at Gina's knock. Her eyes slid from Gina's face to the jar Gina held. "What's that?" the nurse asked with interest.

"Someone has cursed her," Gina said. "It's my mother. I can't reach her now; my hands won't reach her." She unscrewed the lid and reached in to show how impossible it was to actually connect with her mother's hands. She could hear her mother faintly yelling.

"Well, all mothers leave," the nurse said. "In one way or another. Isn't that so?"

"She's yelling for help," Gina pointed out.

The nurse sighed. "I'm here to give help, it's true. But your mother's obviously been cursed, and there's no conventional cure for a curse, especially an unconventional curse." She jiggled the jar, stuck her thumb quickly on her tongue and made motions as if she were paging through a manual in the air. "Yes," she said finally. "This is a tough one to cure. Whoever did this curse—the diminishing curse—it's hard to counter. It's very strong. It requires sacrifice."

"I already gave my toes," Gina whispered.

The nurse was surprised. "Why would you do that? What good are toes?"

"The lifeguard required them."

"He's a fetishist, that's all. He'll probably carry them in his mouth for a month and then spit them out. I never can understand people like him, asking trades for nothing. Well, when you ask something, you risk something." She looked at Gina.

"What am I risking?" Gina asked quickly. "To get my mother back?"

"You may not get what you request; you may get more than you request; you may get something other than what you request; or you may get nothing at all. But nothing changes without a choice."

Gina peered at the jar in which her mother faintly sank. "What will you require from me?"

"I need a strip of your skin," she said.

"How much skin is that?"

"Why, all of it," the nurse said, surprised. "One continuous strip of all your skin, starting under your right armpit and going up and down until it's as long as a river. That's the sympathetic part of it—the river and the water your mother is in; it's a way to reach her. You hang the skin into the jar and your mother will grab onto it and be pulled to the top."

Gina was aghast. "But my skin! What will I do without my skin? And do you give it back to me once we get my mother back?"

"Oh, no, of course not—magic doesn't work on *lending* things; it works on giving things. I'll keep it of course, because I use the skin for medicinal purposes." Here she opened the bottom filing drawer and Gina could see bundles of tightly wrapped skin (like rolls of cellophane) in Ziploc bags.

"I'll give you an ointment, of course," the nurse concluded. "It will only sting at first."

And it stung terribly, and seemed to go on for a terribly long time, but eventually the nurse had the whole roll of skin gathered up, and she put a drop of ointment under Gina's chin. It seemed to cover her body immediately and indeed the sting went away, although there was a residual sense of stickiness, whether from the ointment or from the missing layer of skin, Gina could not tell.

She tried not to look at her skinless hand—red and white in an unpleasant sort of way—as she picked up her mother's jar and unscrewed the lid. "The skin," she whispered, and the nurse obliged, handing it to her rolled up as a ball of yarn.

Gina unrolled it slowly. And lovingly. This was herself, a strange sensation: her former self. Her armor against the world. The border between her and it.

She put the jar on the desk and unrolled her skin so that it tipped into the jar, dipping slowly, very slowly, into her mother's world.

She had to squint to see her skin once it hit the perspective of the jar, being very thin and barely visible. But she lowered it and saw it curl along the top of the water. It didn't have enough weight to actually dip in. She raised it up and out. "What can I put on it to make it go into the water?" she whispered.

"Put it into your mouth and wet it with your tongue," the nurse said. "Nothing would get a mother hooked more than the kiss from a daughter. Trust me, she'll go for it."

Gina took her own skin, the very tip of it, and put it on her tongue. It felt fragile, and thin, exactly as expected. She moistened it with her saliva and then she took it out and kissed it.

"That will work!" the nurse promised.

But it didn't. Her mother reached for it—Gina would swear to that—but she couldn't reach far enough. Instead, bubbles rose from her mouth to the surface. Inside each bubble, Gina was sure, were her mother's cries: "Help me, Gina! Help me!"

She lifted up the skin and lowered it again. Five times: down and up; pause, down and up. The nurse cheered her on: "You're almost there!" she said. "This time will work!"

Finally, Gina gave up. She lowered her head. Her mind was almost numb; her body throbbed and her heart was sore

"Oh well," the nurse said. "We took a chance."

Gina raised her head. "What chance did you take?" she asked.

The nurse flushed. "I lose, too, when the healing doesn't work. But I feel I owe you something—or it's just that I have a good heart. I have a lifetime spent in undoing things like this; if I can't get you to reach her, then the spell is particularly strong. I can give you a referral." She stepped over to her desk, leaning down to a small cylinder, which she spun quickly. "Ah, here it is. Dr. Ramona, Transplants."

"Transplants?" Gina said weakly

"Well, of course. Your mother doesn't have the will to reach your hand. We must transplant some into her. That's obvious." She nodded vigorously to herself, handing the card to Gina, who took up the salve, her mother's jar, and the card, and walked carefully out the door.

Luckily, Dr. Ramona was nearby, behind a mall with sales on lots of glittery things. There was no one in the waiting room (which concerned Gina, but she felt resigned to it; no one could help her; what did it matter?).

She was ushered into an exam room.

"What is it?" the doctor asked. She wore a short white cotton jacket over her clothes. Her name was sewn onto her pocket.

Gina held her mother out to her. The doctor took the jar, squinting, considering. She took her time. She tapped the jar, she tipped it; she unscrewed the lid and stuck a wooden tongue depressor into it; she listened with her stethoscope.

"I've seen this once before," she said finally.

"And what happened?"

The doctor drew her lips in tightly. "I'm sorry," she said. "This is not a deliberate curse; it's a random one. The person who did this isn't even aware. That makes it harder to counter it. In essence, there's nothing to counter. No animosity, no anger, no feelings at all. There was no intent; it just happened. A stray curse."

Gina sat there. It was so quiet that the faint ring of her mother's cries could be heard, even from as far away as within the jar.

"My mother is calling for help," Gina whispered.

"Yes," the doctor said. "I would too."

Even that simple agreement cheered Gina. The doctor understood.

"What about a transplant? The nurse said something about a transplant."

The minutes ticked as the doctor was silent. She pursed her lips, she loosened them; her eyes roamed, her eyes came back; she lifted her hand; she put it down. "There might be some hope there," she agreed quietly. "Some small hope. But it's such a risk, and there's so much to lose."

"I think she's lost just about everything already," Gina argued.

"I didn't mean for her; there's not much left for her to lose. I meant for you. Sometimes a curse is stronger because the victim has no will to survive. A kind of compromised immune system, if you will; immunity being the desire to live. We could take yours and give it to her—but you see the danger, don't you? If we take yours away?"

Gina saw it, definitely. If she gave her own desire to live to her mother, then what would be left for her? It was a sickening prospect, really. She wanted her own life, certainly; was that selfish and cruel? Her eyes strayed to the jar with her mother in it, which the doctor had set down on the table. The doctor waited intently.

"What success rate?" Gina whispered.

"Very small."

"Then why do it? Why take the chance?"

"I wouldn't advise it, myself. I wouldn't do it, myself. We don't really understand curses like this. Impersonal, indifferent, lacking passion— they can't be broken easily because we don't know what was offered to make the curse, so we can't offer more. It's irrational. That's the problem. When you have an irrational curse, there's very little hope." She waited to see if Gina would say anything. "The ones who survived may have survived accidentally."

Gina's eyes were on the jar. "She's suffering."

"She is. But we have no proof that she *knows* she's suffering. That part of her may be gone. At least, we can hope so."

Gina took her mother's jar. She walked down the long street back to her mother's house. She walked slowly, because she didn't have her toes to take some of the burden off her feet. She held the jar in her hands, but the jar often slipped because there was no skin to keep her body fluids from seeping out. Her body was weeping. She tipped the jar every which way, but no matter what position it was in, her mother was still below the water, still reaching up, still calling faintly.

Her mother's house was the last house before the wilderness. It was a thing her mother often spoke about, the wilderness, though there was nothing in particular Gina could recall about it—not her mother's wishes concerning it, not whether it was frightening or soothing. It was just a thing her mother mentioned now and then, the wilderness.

Gina stood at its edge. She was silent and listened for a long long time. She didn't know if her mother could hear her—her mother hadn't answered her so far, and it seemed she couldn't change what she was saying. Forever and ever, she could call out, "Help me, Gina" and forever and ever, Gina would not.

Before the sun set, when the birds took their last song, Gina raised her arm and flung the jar as far as she could into the wilderness—so far that she would be unable to find it; so far that she couldn't hear it; so far that only another jar, flung exactly the same way, would land next to it and add its own unrelenting cry. She would leave instructions for her own daughter, if it should happen to her. Fling my jar far and high and long, she imagined herself writing as she turned to walk down the road to her own house: let me go.

# ACKNOWLEDGEMENTS

"Searching for Penny" was originally published in *American Literary Review* and the collection *Clockworm* by Tartarus Press; "Ball Lightning" was published in *Oxmag* and in *Best of the Web 2009*; "Sick Leave" in *Alaska Quarterly Review*; "Frankie the Mob" in *Southword*; "Road Work" in *Phoebe*; "That Place" in *Maine Review*; Cora in *Short Édition*; "The Terrible Journey" in *Michigan Quarterly Review*; "Bright Bright Bedlam" in *Kenyon Review*; "The Year of His Father" in *Michigan Quarterly Review*.